A SEASON IN SINJI

J.L.Carr

THE QUINCE TREE PRESS
BURY ST EDMUNDS

A Season in Sinji

First published in 1967 by Alan Ross Ltd.,
(London Magazine Editions); subsequently by
Quartet and Penguin

This edition published by

The Quince Tree Press

2003

Copyright © R.D. Carr

ISBN 1-904016-08-1

The Novels of J.L. Carr:

All available in Quince Tree Press Editions
www.quincetreepress.co.uk

'Reflections' & 'Songbirds' by Joan Hassall; other illustrations are by the author or
Thomas Bewick

This is a Printing Office,
Cross-roads of Civilisation,
Refuge of all the Arts against the Ravages of Time.
From this place Words may fly abroad
Not to perish as Waves of Sound but fix'd in Time,
Not corrupted by the hurrying Hand but verified in Proof.
Friend, you are on Safe Ground;
This is a Printing Office

Printed in Great Britain by
Stanley L. Hunt (Printers) Ltd, Rushden, Northamptonshire

'The game of cricket is thoroughly British ... Every manoeuvre must be tried in a desperate state of the game. Endeavour by every means in your power - such as by changing the bowling, by little alterations in the field, or by any excuse you can invent - *to delay the time, that the strikers may become cold and inactive. And when the turn is in your favour you may push the game: but even then be not flushed with success, but your play be still cool, cautious and steady.'*

John Nyren, Hambledon 1793.
'Hints to Captains.'

One

I particularly remember one evening at Blackfen. Wakerly
and I hadn't money left for the flicks and were pretending
to drink W.V.S. tea, sitting in the bay window of a decaying
vicarage dragged back to life for the Duration. It was lashing
down—more even than its Lancashire usual—when down
the drive, between the sooty laurels, marched this blonde,
page-boy hair styling down to her shoulders, black jumper
moulded round a really promising bust, grey slacks and an
open scarlet mac flapping around her thighs. She glittered.

Then, in this weather for wellingtons, I saw that she
wasn't wearing shoes. Only sodden silk stockings. She
homed straight in over the gravel and through the pools and
puddles and, after her, a private soldier paddled at a half-
trot. She crossed the canteen in long strides, leaving heel
and ball prints on the brown lino, glanced scornfully at us
(she must have noticed Wakerly hopefully whip off his
steel-rimmed spectacles) and shook the rain from her hair.
She was a marvellous looker, officer fodder, and, when she
spoke, it was like an aristocrat. Not like the female abori-
ginees of Blackfen & District.

The man padded humbly in after her and bought two teas.
Even in his thick-soled boots the top of his head only came
up to her nose. Then she began to slang the slosh in a very
loud voice, describing it (rightly) as disgusting dishwater.
Everybody stopped talking and the W.V.S. women (doing
their bit for the boys) smouldered (but didn't wither her).
And her little man obediently nodded his head (but drank
it). Then she shoved her cup back at him and stalked off into

the downpour, leaving him to shuffle guiltily to the counter and, then, after her.

Like a film trailer, it had no ending. And no meaning. No, that's untrue: it was a detail from a bigger picture, a flurry in the crowd watching a game. (And, anyway, I did see her just once more . . . in Africa, glaring insolently at me from a bundle of yellowing Daily Mirrors.) Put it like this— you're fielding in the deep, the boundary's edge, and, for a moment and for no reason at all, you catch the glance of someone you'll never see again. But, for that brief moment, you're part of each other's life. This whole business, from start to end, was like that, like a game of cricket, the issue never sure, who'd win, who'd lose, and there were some, like these, who watched momentarily and went away. And others who prodded around, doing what they could but not really knowing what it was all about; I mean not understanding what was at stake as will was pitted against will, as we waited for the change of luck that always comes, watched for a grip to slacken as the game turned. . . . That spectator, the one in the red mac, disappeared into the rain.

Rain fell every day during those last weeks at Blackfen. We were waiting to be pushed off overseas so it suited our mood and, anyway, we scarcely stirred from the huts; awful as they were, at least the roofs didn't leak. But Wakerly was marooned half a mile away in the tent compound which he complained was awash. I used to meet him three times a day in the cookhouse so I heard it three times daily. Even though it was well known that the RAF treated its overseas drafts like stray dogs in a police pound, his story sounded unlikely. But I couldn't check on it because my boots let in water. As he described it, you'd have imagined he lodged on a fishing fleet.

'Part of it falls from above, and part of it seeps up with the sewage,' he explained. 'One lot gurgles, and the other

8

laps.' (He had a slight stammer, especially over 'l', so he said 'l-laps'. *They*'re readying us for the Boat. It's their Diabolical System.'

That was a laugh. If there was any system in the RAF, then it worked on teacakes. At Blackfen (their press-gang branch) what passed for planning was plotting. But I got his point.

'Bl-l-ackfen-in-Lancasheer,' he said, mimicking the locals' twang. 'L-lancasheer! My God! And the brightest gem in its diadem—Blackfen-on-Manchester Ship Canal! Just grind it out slowly and you hear all that needs saying about Lanca-sheer, Bacup, the Brontes and Blackburn Rovers. With this dump thrown in.'

'Oh, it's not all that bad,' I said. 'It's only a transit camp. And the Brontes were Yorkshire.' (I knew that be-cause Grandad used to go on about them.)

'Hell's a transit camp,' he replied, 'and the climate's better.' This was just his way of talking: he meant half he said. It was an act like his appearance. Although he was tall and stooped, he wasn't anything like as clumsy as he made himself out to be. The same with his round service specs which he always wore, though I knew he had an expensive pair, tortoiseshell rims, not imitation. I always believed that he could switch his flat feet and his stammer on and off as it suited him. Sometimes I thought he did it to hide his shame at having to mix in with the grim mob caked together in the bottom layer of the RAF. But, looking back, I think he didn't care that he'd been separated by the War from his own sort. In this snob-ridden land, and especially down south, there aren't many like he was. When he weighed up folks, class and education didn't go into the balance.

We were more than mates; he could have been a brother. I shall never forget him. Though I let him down in the end.

But, as I said, he exaggerated: Blackfen wasn't as bad as he made out. There were ten miles of barbed wire to keep us in, but there were gaps in it so wide that men rode in and out on bicycles. In fact, there was a story going round that, on the far side, beyond walking distance of all but health fiends subduing their sex-drive by violent exercise, there was a hole so big that you could drive a motor car through it. And I personally knew of a massive cast-iron gate tied up with a piece of binder twine.

Of course, nobody wanted to go overseas. After a Churchill broadcast, for a day or two there might be a stirring to rush into the breach. But it passed. Most of the time we kept up our spirits by reminding ourselves that we were all right so far and used to shamble off to congregate in lavatories, anywhere warm, to boast about jolly dispersal-points on distant aerodromes or such and such a cookhouse where we had a Special Arrangement, places where we were *somebody*. Always past things. Mercifully, the future was hidden from us, but we supposed it would be unpleasant and maybe dangerous. And one thing we knew for certain: the War would go on for years yet and, once they'd pressganged us on to the Boat, we'd not see U.K. again for four, five, maybe six years.

I needn't have been there myself. I could have stayed farming which was a reserved occupation and, because my grandad was in his late sixties, I'd have had a cast-iron case. But my mother had persuaded him to let a couple of upstairs rooms to a navigator at one of the bomber stations up the Vale, an oldish man called Bellenger who we got to like and have in for the odd meal. One Sunday, we took a walk up to Gormire from the back of our land, and he said, 'Tom, I'm going to give you some advice. If you don't watch, you're going to stay here until they carry you out. Now I like your grandfather, but he's a different generation. And he likes his own way and gets it. Unless you get away for a year or two, you'll never find out who you are.'

When I signed up, my grandad made a fuss as I'd expected. He was an overbearing man, and that was one of the reasons, I suppose, my dad left home before I remembered him.

Nothing really happened at Blackfen. We got up as late as we dared without missing breakfast and then hurried back to lie on our beds, staring at the billet ceiling, stunned by non-stop dance songs from the loudspeakers. These were set permanently at FULL VOLUME and couldn't be turned off. Wakerly said that they even planted them on high posts ('above high-tide mark') in the tent compound. 'It's p-part of their diabolical plot—to drown your thoughts,' he told me.

It must have been no more than the lads from the factories were used to, but at our house all music not hymns or cantatas had come under the general heading of Rubbish, and I was in no shape at all for this assault: it battered its way into my brain. Even now, twenty years later, I can sing all the words, verses and choruses of two or three of them— 'My spurs go jingle-jangle-jingle', 'I'm dreaming of a White Christmas' and 'There'll always be an England' . . .

> 'There'll always be an England
> While there's a country lane,
> A cottage dreaming 'neath its thatch
> Beside a field of grain.'

Everybody in the billet used to yell it (me too), but find me the erk who believed it applied to him in person: nobody wanted the bother of shoring up U.K.'s thatched cottages or even council houses, if it meant Overseas Service to do it. This, I supposed, was part of the process Mr. Bellenger had recommended to Find out who You are.

They didn't push us around. Really, there wasn't anything for us to do except eat, sleep and be around each mid-

11

night waiting for The Call. I fancy we were reckoned to be Desperate Men with nothing to lose but our Chains.

On one or two afternoons each week wandering lecturers were brought in to rally us. Now they were men. They bashed away with glassy grins about badgers, Ben Jonson and the Britain We Were Fighting For. Personally, I could always see a bit of education might come in useful, but Wakerly said that university had done only one thing for him—to make him information-repellent. Yet I noticed that he always made me sit with him near the front. (Further back, the information-resistance barrage was 100% effective.)

I particularly remember one pair of these minstrels. Whilst the robot partner, a middle-aged woman made up to look gorgeous, worked a record-player, the frontman did the patter, his ploy, boiled down, being to convince his hearers that Laurence Olivier read verses better than most other people. All that was to follow hung on that, so he had the corporal order some dimwit on to the stage to be hidden behind a screen with his beautiful partner and her machinery.

'Now,' we were told, 'you are going to hear two renderings of the same immortal lines and then I shall want *you* to tell *me* in which way the poet (were he here) would have wanted his immortal lines said.'

Actually, up till then, it was pretty quiet because the erks thought they might be about to witness a conjuring trick (because of the screen). Then, a thick Liverpudlian voice began. Honestly, it was a foreign language. (In the North Riding we're outlandish, but they say you can always tell what we mean.) But this was a cave man cranching dinosaur bones.

Then this actor on a gramophone record said it. I don't know who wrote it or where it came from: in fact, I only remember one line because, for once, it lodged and, also, because Wakerly repeated it—once at Blackfen and once in Africa.

'Now,' said this frontman, 'you don't need *me* to ask bright chaps like *you* which one sounded *right* though your mate did Very Well Let's Give Him a Clap ...'

'The first one ... the first!' everybody yelled. Even Wakerly. I mean to say this was crazy: I was utterly disgusted. Even if you could compare that foul Lancasheer rant with English properly spoken, it still had to be the second, the man on the gramophone, just to fit in with the man's plan. That was the way he'd planned it and I respect people who plan. Half the world's trouble is because there's no plan and we lose half the Test Matches for the same reason. . . .

But they kept shouting 'The first one ... the first!' and, when the cave man stumbled from behind the screen, they shrieked and shouted as though he'd just shot the winning goal in a cup final. It went on and on. The corporals rushed in from their quiet cups of tea and formed up across the front to menace us. But every time this lecturer opened his mouth (still keeping up his knowing smile), the uproar exploded—'The first one ... the first!'

The poor chap went white, took out his handkerchief and began to blot up the sweat. Then a sergeant jumped on to the stage, shouted at him and he turned blindly, running with shoulders hunched, as if the shouting was actually *hitting* him. He left all his kit behind. Then they turned all the loudspeakers FULL VOLUME ('There'll always be an England, While there's a country lane . . .') and drove us out into the rain.

Outside, Wakerly sobered down: I expect he felt ashamed of letting down what, basically, were his own sort. He looked depressed.

'He was right,' he said.

'Who was?'

' "The b-bitter, old and wrinkled truth." He was right—

13

the man who wrote it. We've had it. I'm twenty-four and you're a couple of years older, and both of us have had it. If we live till we're thirty, it'll be a miracle. We've had the best of it, already. At Budmouth.'

'Well, I'm going to hang on,' I said. 'You too; we're not aircrew.'

But I could see that he wasn't listening. I'd seen him like this before, at Budmouth, when he knew in his heart that he'd lost her to Turton. And, once he began to brood over Caroline Driffield, it was no use talking to him. Frankly, remembering her, I didn't feel too talkative myself. So I shut up.

It was at Budmouth that I'd first met Wakerly. They'd sent a batch of us there to be camp coal-heavers, lavatory cleaners, mess orderlies, dustmen. And he and I were set to collecting salvage for the War Effort—card, paper, aluminium, scrap-iron, anything that could be pulped or melted and used again. Our staple trade was airframes because it was a training station for Doncasters which, in their heyday, before they were found out, slew more Englishmen than ever they did Germans. They used to dive in left, right and centre, scattering their bits and pieces over a terrified countryside for us to pick up. 'We're instant archaeologists,' Wakerly used to say.

I reckon we could have stayed there for the Duration. It wasn't worth while posting us, we hadn't a trade, and we were doing filthy jobs no-one else wanted: we were camp furniture. Personally, I had no complaints. I'd scooped out a nice little niche for myself with the town's cricket club (which still played games) and made several fifties. (I'd have continued to the hundred on one or two of these occasions against the horrible bowling of the village veterans but, during the War, it was put about that you were unpatriotic if you stayed long after fifty.)

The great drawback was that, with petrol rationed, they used sheep to keep the grass down and, though a batsman was compensated for their inefficiency up front (you had to loft the ball to score a boundary) by their bounty behind (fielders didn't care to dive for the ball), I'd have expected better from a place the size of Budmouth. At home, below the Hambledon Hills, you couldn't expect much : we were short of level fields. The meadow we used was as big as a prairie : I can remember only *one* boundary ever being scored. Just think of that. Every blessed run *had* to be run. On three sides the boundary was a hawthorn hedge close on a hundred yards away over rough grass and the fourth side was at the top of the field, so far away that the farmer's daughter (a tall, mangy creature I used to dream about when I was fifteen) looked no more than a blur as she watched from the field gate. . . .

However, to get back to Budmouth, once I was clear of the aerodrome and the salvage wagon, I got settled in there and built up a bit of a reputation, so that quite a few folks called me Mr. Flanders.

You may wonder why I'm dwelling on this and going back a couple of years to do it. But what happened at Budmouth is the nub, the whole point of the story : everything stemmed from there or rather from Caroline Driffield, because that's where we met her. And Turton, too, of course.

It happened like this. In the evenings, Wakerly and I used to pub-crawl round the district. Not for any wish of mine because I'd signed the pledge half-a-dozen times but found it embarrassing drinking lemonade. To me, just walking round the country, without calling at pubs, was pleasure enough. Anyway, to give purpose to our trips, he (Wakerly) did a little drawing of each establishment we visited and, later, transferred them to a map he'd made which he called A Guide to Safe Boozing in Budmouth & Environs. Then he tinted them and, in indian ink, below, wrote a couple of

15

lines. I still have it—framed: his mother gave it to me. It's so unusual that people ask me about it, but I can't bring myself to talk casually about it or him or Budmouth or Sinji —you'd need to tell everything if you told anything.

But to give you some idea—

> 'At Coulters Ash avoid The Bell:
> They've joined the beer tap to the well.'

and 'The Swan at Forder's by the water.
> It hires punts and the landlord's daughter.'

But, for Budmouth itself he put . . . and, even now, I can hardly bear to read it,

> 'A guardian angel tends The Vine—
> Sweetest of girls . . . dear Caroline.'

This Vine wasn't in the middle of the town. It faced the sea, looking across on to the quay, and it had been a spot for mariners to drop a first and farewell pint when they arrived from and returned to the perils of the deep. That is, until the brewers had made it a really awful phoney. And now you either built up a back-ache on the half-size beer barrels in the Chart Room or nibbled polite cheese sandwiches in The Galley or, if you were out of the local top drawer, had an invitation into the Fo'c'sle. The genuine ocean-going article had been warned off by threepence extra on a pint.

She was tall for a girl and, though her hair was almost ash-blonde, was unusually dark-skinned. Whenever I looked at her, I thought of bits of The Song of Solomon read guiltily whilst Wesleyan local preachers raved away through their false teeth,

> 'I am black but I am comely
> O ye daughters of Jerusalem . . .'

I think it was her eyes which were wide apart and slanted

rather, or maybe her mouth which had a bruised look with a hint of perspiration on the upper lip. Or the way, standing, she bent slightly backwards, which threw up her breasts and drew your mind down through the darkness,

> 'The joints of my thighs are like jewels,
> My navel is like a round goblet,
> My belly like a heap of wheat. . . .'

None of the girls at our chapel were like that: they either smelt of sweat or they giggled.

But it was her eyes chiefly I remember. It was hard to say what colour they were. I used to wonder what it would be like when you were alone with her, very close, and looking into them. It seemed about the least likely thing that could ever happen to me.

Yet she dressed with great modesty, in quiet colours. [As did my mother.] Outside The Vine, she wore tailor-made tweed suits: the one I best remember had a little velvet collar.

It boils down to this: she had style. You either have or you haven't. That's all there is to it; it's beyond doubt. Herbert Sutcliffe had it; Edgar Oldroyd, for all his runs in the score-books, didn't. I think I can say that, in those days, on the right wicket against good bowling, I had it myself. It's nothing you can pick up from a cricket book or a ladies' magazine. It's like that man in the Old Testament who says casually, 'The Spirit of the Lord is upon me,' and added under his breath, 'And you can take it or leave it, that's the way it is.' But she wasn't for me: she was out of my class. She was for the Wakerlys and Turtons.

> 'Set me a seal upon thine heart,
> For love is strong as death,
> Jealousy cruel as the grave.'

Well, at least I knew it.

I had very little experience of girls then. If you've lived in a village, you know that it's fatal to go out with a local girl. Everybody—particularly relations—has you fixed up to marry her and, honestly, in the farming districts, the choice is so restricted and the shame of being left on the shelf so dreadful, that, even if she's not struck all that much on you, give a girl the chance and she sticks like a limpet. In any case, I knew I didn't want to marry *anybody*: I wanted something a bit different, someone with a bit of style, and I was ready to wait for her. So I lacked experience, nerve, cheek, whatever you call it. Though class and snobbery disgusted me, I couldn't forget them and I guessed Caroline Driffield might look very differently at me if she thought for a minute I might be serious about her.

Sometimes I wondered if everyone was like me. Most people were. I knew that. But was everybody? In stories, there were kings who married beggar-maids. But in real life? And women? Were they ruled by Class when it came down to brass tacks, to love or lust or whatever decided folks that they could share a house with a man for a lifetime? Or was there a wild streak in them that didn't give a tuppenny blast who the man was so long as he took their fancy?

From what happened later, I learnt a lot of the answers but, then, it was too late.

Wakerly had gone overboard for her. He didn't say so: that wouldn't have been Wakerly. But I could see, watching his face as they talked over the bar. And I could see, too, that she knew as well. It didn't surprise me really. They both spoke southern lah-di-dah, had been to boarding schools, looked at you in the same cool way.

But he didn't go far enough fast enough. That was his mistake and, later on, he knew it. It wasn't the time for good old village courting any more—where everybody knew it was your girl and kept his distance as you made your leisurely way to the wedding. These were here-today-and-gone-

18

tomorrow days; life was concertinered. In any case, even if there'd been all the time in the world, once you're sure, then settle it one way or the other, win or lose. There's never as much time as you think.

Her parents had been killed in a London air-raid and her uncle, an officer in the Naval Reserve, was at sea, having left Caroline's aunt (who was a silly, flighty sort of woman) in charge. They had a system of mirrors which revealed thirsty customers in the different bars and, in between times, Caroline would come to rest near Wakerly and me. What did we talk about? Frankly, I wasn't with it half the time, but she'd flash me the occasional smile and he'd refer to something going on in the camp. And there was always cricket to fall back on. She was the only girl or woman I ever knew who understood it properly. Up home, they only pretended to. Though it's only fair to say they got precious little encouragement: most Yorkshiremen behave to their women as though they were back in the Book of Deuteronomy.

She showed me the score-cards she'd kept from days at Lords (and was properly impressed when I told her Thomas Lord was a Thirsk man—it's on the Vale, no more than a dozen miles from our farm). She knew how to work a full-sized score-book and you couldn't catch her on M.C.C. rules. She even knew W. G. Grace's extra one—'Braces are *not* worn.' It was quite extraordinary when you come to think of it.

It was spring then and, on Sunday afternoons, all three of us and her terrier used to go walking on the downs behind the town. The other two used to laugh a lot but there was no mushy stuff, kissing and dearests and darlings. Perhaps there should have been. But, once, when we came up to a field-gate, where the wild daffs grew by a hedge that needed felling and laying again, I remember she slipped her little gloved hand into his. 'Peter,' she said, 'say something for

19

us to remember it by . . . spring . . . today . . . being young . . . before we forget . . .'

It was a warm day; the sun was shining. One of those clear bright days when the greenness makes this the loveliest country in the world. Yet, when she'd said it, I felt a chill, as though age had touched me. I suppose it was the way she put it—'before we forget.' Was there so long to come—when we *might* forget? And a time when these two would be together and I would be on my own?

'Before we forget?' Wakerly said quietly. 'But I don't want to forget, Caroline. (He'd never called her anything before that.) I shan't forget. This is a day I'll remember. You and Tom . . . being with friends . . .'

(Why didn't he say it then? 'I love you.' It would have settled everything and I'd have known one way or the other. And what happened, needn't have happened. But he didn't. He just did as he was told.)

It came without him turning a hair . . .

' "Before it is too late, before we forget
The cherry white in the woods and the curdled clouds,
And the lapwing crying low above the plough." '

I don't know to this day who made it up and he said he didn't know either when, later, I got him to write it down for me.

She was right in one thing though: a day like that never came again. Things seemed to go wrong from then on. In fact, only a night or two after that, when Wakerly was in camp on fire-picket, I was leaving The Vine when Caroline asked me to wait a minute because she wanted a breath of air. So I stood in the black-out until she followed me, her camel coat over her shoulders and tying a silk scarf under her chin.

We'd scarcely gone a dozen paces when she took my hand.

20

'You're not annoyed with me because I've come with you?' she said.

'No,' I said. 'I was just surprised, that's all.'

When we reached the edge of town, she stopped by a field-gate. 'Perhaps I'd better not go any further,' she said.

'You're right,' I told her, 'it's far enough: there's not many folks about.'

'When shall I be seeing you again?'

'I'm on the flarepath tomorrow but Wakerly will . . .'

'I said *you*. Not Peter. When shall I be seeing *you*?'

'I'll be coming on Friday with . . .'

'Don't you *ever* do anything on your own?' (she sounded on edge).

This was getting beyond me and I shuffled my feet. 'Well,' I said, 'the time's getting on. Perhaps you'd better be getting back. I'll be saying Goodnight . . .'

'Then say it properly,' she said, and took both my arms and pulled me against the gate. She was breathing quickly and her mouth was open and her hands groped till she seemed to melt into me, her head well back, her eyes were closed but not looking as I'd imagined it might be.

'We can't here,' she muttered. 'Let's change to the field.' And she pulled away and began to climb the gate. I caught sight of her face and it wasn't her. I don't believe that she was sure who I was any more and I don't think she cared. I'd never seen a girl like it before: the nearest to it I knew was one of our farm cats in heat, when we tried to shut it up in a grain loft till its ten days were up.

Honestly—well, how can I put it—although I was twenty-five I'd no experience of what I guessed she was after. I'd never done it and was terrified of making a fool of myself so I caught at her wrist.

'Look, Caroline,' I said. 'Not now. I've got to go or I'll be on a charge. Look, I *have* to go.'

And then, ridiculously, I added lamely, 'Next time. . . .'

She turned and slid back. Her eyes were dilated, she was breathing fast.

'Goodnight,' I said, and tried to kiss her. She looked at me as though she'd never seen me before, a bitter look as if she was hurt. Then she walked straight past. It was about the worst thing that ever happened to me and I turned and half ran off into the darkness, feeling as if my inside was coming out.

Probably unbelievable. But true. There *are* people who don't spend every waking hour planning the best way to jump into a girl's bed. Some because the sap is sluggish, some because they're inexperienced and fear being a fool. I think I was a mixture of all three; but, chiefly, the last.

Where it went wrong between Wakerly and her I don't know. Perhaps there was nothing. Perhaps she just moved away from him. But for me, it was *then*, that night by the gate. She was a girl who'd become a woman and, at twenty-five, I was still a boy. I know now what I should have done. But, then, it happened too quickly, without warning, on her impulse.

And that wasn't *me*: unless I could work to a plan, think ahead, then it was domino for me.

And Turton had that sort of thing all worked out, cut and dried, from top to bottom, from A to Z. And so he won.

We knew this Leading Aircraftsman Turton by sight because he worked in the Watch Office and was usually around plotting positions of bits of Doncasters before we picked them up. And we knew he was loathed by the photographers, who had to follow him and, when he told them, take pictures of twisted props and half-buried engines. He'd let them know (casually) that he had—amongst other comforts for the troops—a mistress in London. One of them used to mimic him . . . 'A youngish divorcée, old boy, runs a little boutique off Bond Street. Makes a mint. Doesn't cost me a penny. Bit older than me, of course. But fully ripened, well trained. Grateful for anything. Clings rather. Must shake her off soon. But she does for the moment . . .' And, though they'd never admit it, these photographers disliked him most because he knew more about their own job than they did.

Most of them had been studio assistants (weddings and what not) but he'd been a director of his dad's milling business and was a keen weekend photographer. But he knew his stuff all right: in fact, he had a better all-round grasp of it than the pros because he was more intelligent. He was good all right, he was so damned smart that he despised the rest of us and, later, when the chance came, rode us down roughshod. He valued men at their face value. Wakerly and I were salvage-wallahs so we must think and act like salvage-wallahs—that's the way his mind worked—and we must be kicked around like salvage-wallahs. That was Turton. You're going to hear plenty about him before I've done.

He had reddish hair, not quite ginger, and was good-looking in his way. Everything was right about him except his nose, which was just a bit too long. And his eyes . . . he could let them go out of focus so as to look at you and, at the same time, let you know you weren't registering.

I remember him first on a day when it was lashing down, the rain soaking in from the sea to drive us into the Naffy, huddled in those ridiculous groundsheets smelling of baby's bed-rubber, which shamed everyone who ever wore one (except the army); they had a big brown button at the neck and the rain dribbled down their decaying ginger sides into your boot tops. Well, there we were, lepers in our dirt, sucking up our tea to make it outlast the rain, when in came this Turton wearing an elegant, long gas-cape. It had four press studs, sleeves and even a collar of sorts. They were only to be worn during a mustard gas attack though they were ideal for this weather. So we looked at him out of our eye-corners and hated him because he had more nerve than the rest of us

23

and wouldn't be put down. And he was talking lah-di-dah, loudly, like that marvellous blonde in the W.V.S. canteen. And, naturally, he smoked his fag from a holder.

Once you'd seen him, you remembered: he stood out. His reddish hair? Dead pale face? Eyes which saw you and then didn't? The air of absolute unquestioning superiority he gave himself? You remembered him for all those things rolled into one. And something else. But hard to say *what*. You just *felt* it.

I remembered the evening Turton first found The Vine. He stood for a moment at the door, taking it in, seeing and admiring Caroline. And then he moved forward and more or less took over. It never can have occurred to him that she might not have preferred his company. We were—salvage-wallahs. Utter confidence is everything when you're playing to win. Everything! (I've seen it on a bowler's face and then you have to beat him, really let him see the middle of the bat, crack down with all your weight on his mistakes, break him. He knows it, the field knows it, even back in the pavilion they know it: it's will against will: it's what makes cricket the game like no other game.) But she was only eighteen and hadn't experience to see through him. And we'd disappointed her. And maybe she really wasn't the girl we wanted her to be. So he took over. It was as simple as that.

After that, we found him there every evening.

It hit Wakerly hard but he didn't say anything. And, after a while, we stopped going to The Vine and began on the map again. But the heart had gone out of it.

One morning I met Caroline in town and, tactfully, wasn't seeing her, but she stopped me.

'Hullo Tom,' she said, 'I don't see much of you nowadays.'

'No,' I said, 'I don't get into town so often.'

'And how's Peter?'

I made up some story but could see that she didn't believe me. Since then, I've often wondered what would have happened had I replied, 'Peter? He's in love with you, Caroline. Like me. And we can't bear to watch you listening to all the glib things Wakerly's too straight-forward to say—and I daren't after you know when ... but you're my kind of girl for all the difference in our homes. It would be wonderful to walk with you down Wintersghyll Street or sit across from you at the table up at the farm. It's your eyes I think. No, it's all of you ... You'd have been all right with me ...

Set me as a seal upon thy heart, As a seal upon thine arm.

For love is as strong as death, jealousy as the grave ...'

What would she have said to that rot, out there on the busy footpath, among the shops, in Budmouth?

No, I'd missed my chance at the gate and I didn't get another. And Wakerly drew back, declared before he'd scarcely taken his stand. (Or so I thought at that time.)

'Oh well,' she said, 'do drop in and keep in touch.' Then she smiled and walked away. I only saw her once again.

I didn't tell Wakerly that I'd met her. In fact we never mentioned her again [but for that once at Blackfen and the night before he died at Sinji].

To take my mind off it, I joined the local cricket club.

The Secretary/Captain was keeping the club ticking over, tiding it through the War. He was an estate agent but looked as though he still trusted everybody. He limped from a horse's kick and used to call me Mr. Flanders and I called him Mr. Ridd, but everyone else called him Harold. Some folks you take to straight off: I did to Mr. Ridd and he to me. We both knew we *understood* the game and it didn't make any difference at all to either of us that we came from different ends of the country.

'Another of your chaps has been asking for a game,' he told me one Saturday, 'and I've fixed him up for next week. Can you let him know; his name's Turton.'

I said that I didn't know him and explained the Station was as big as a small town with men coming and going all the time, and suggested that a post card would find him.

On the Saturday, Mr. Ridd introduced me and we nodded as though we'd never seen one another before. I didn't need to speak again because, when he found one or two fellows had been to boarding schools, he put on the Old Boy act and the phoney moth-eaten passwords began to patter round the changing room . . . Agars Plough, Free Foresters, Cryptics, fast bowlers became 'quickies', a pint of mild became 'a noggin of ale'. But it was Turton that was doing all the chattering. The others had to live with 'Harold' and make their livings with all sorts and conditions of Budmouth men during the week. So they detached themselves as quick as they could.

It turned out that he claimed some skill as a bowler so Mr. Ridd gave him three or four overs which I watched with close but biased interest. Wakerly claimed I looked s-sardonic, but that was his exaggeration: I have a natural blank face.

He placed an elaborate field, making delicate adjustments . . . 'just a step over to your left, old man' . . . and when everybody was pegged out on the exact square foot of turf, he began his run-up which was fancy, far too long, ending up with windmilling arms and both feet pedalling the air which, naturally, checked his momentum and ballsed up his rhythm. Talk about the mountain heaving and groaning to squeeze out a mouse! When the balls popped out, they were homely, up-and-down stuff, fairly accurate but dead easy to accommodate if you took your time and sorted them out. And they were a doddle for sloggers of which this village side had eleven such of prime-cut, and these gratefully hammered Turton hard and high all round the ceiling, the balls banging down through the spreading chestnut trees, flushing out wood-pigeons and lovers lying below in the long

26

grass. None of those he'd carefully positioned was in the right place to catch the rockets when eventually Newton's Law brought them down, because the Laws of Cricket rightly rule that batsmen caught on the wrong side of the boundary are not-out.

So Mr. Ridd sent him no more cards. 'Between you and me, Mr. Flanders,' he said, 'and in the strictest confidence, it's nothing to do with the runs they knocked off him because those silly sods from Hengistbury, as is well known for many generations in these parts, can only hit good length stuff; you have to bowl short of a length to get 'em out, the sort of ball a chap like yourself (and me, in my prime) would properly pull to the leg boundary. These peasants would be just as likely to do the same to your own George Macaulay. No, it was just his *manner*. Round here, in the West Country, we don't go in for that London Old Boy stuff. Some of us take a glass in the saloon and some in the snug. But there's no "Me up, you down." And I take it, from what I've read, you're that way up north.'

I said we were. [But, though that may have been true of the mill towns in the West Riding, step from your place in the North Riding and you soon get your toes trodden on; it's still the Middle Ages round Malton and Pickering.]

'Now me,' went on Mr. Ridd, 'I attended Blundells—like John Ridd—no relation—but I don't reckon myself any the better for it. There were some real scoundrels there that I wouldn't change a dozen of for one or two lads I know went to council schools...'

[I liked 'Harold'. I'm sorry I shall never see him again. Some men you feel spot on with from the start.]

'Now you, Mr. Flanders,' he said, 'if you don't mind my saying it, I *understand* you. I feel that I've known you for years and I wish you were going to settle in these parts... There's one or two nice little farms....'

It was mutual, you see.

And it heartened me. I felt that Wakerly having thrown in his cards didn't bind me down to hanging my hands. Everybody should have a second chance. And what he (Mr. Ridd) said was enough to stiffen my nerve to go back to The Vine and I went the next Friday about nine. There was no sign of Caroline. I hung about but she didn't show up.

It was nearly closing-time and I was just giving it up and going, when the door from the domestic quarters opened and Turton appeared behind the bar: he must have known I was there.

'Why don't you clear off?' he asked me. 'If you're waiting to see Carol, you're wasting your time. She doesn't want you hanging about. Can't you see when you're not wanted?'

We were on different sides of the counter so I couldn't do anything and, before I could collect my wits, he'd gone.

Out in the black-out again, I walked furiously up and down the pavement. Then I set off back to the camp. I got so far but then I turned back. I felt it was now or never. And what I did next wasn't like me. I'm ashamed of it. All I can say is that I wasn't myself that night.

I went quietly round the back way to The Vine, over a fence and then felt my way across their garden to where there was a light showing from a slight gap in the curtaining. It was Caroline's room and she lay there on the bed, naked (except for a bracelet Wakerly had given her) and face down on a yellow and black coverlet; whilst Turton, only in his service shirt (and tie) lay beside her on his back, one leg bent, knee pointing up, one arm across the small of her back, finger and thumb caressing the leg nearest the window. He was staring at the ceiling and smiling. There was only a table-lamp lit and, except for the bed, the rest of the room was in shadow. They lay like a picture.

I looked for only a moment: it was like a blow in the face. Then I stumbled off, my legs like jelly.

The Watch Office chaps told me what happened after that. Turton asked her uncle's permission to marry his niece (her aunt didn't count). But Uncle could see through him and refused outright, saying that she was too young and her people hadn't spent a mint on her education to end up with her married into Other Ranks. If he got himself a commission, then he might reconsider. . . .

They said that Turton was white with rage when he let it out. (He must have been or he never would.) 'Who does he think he is!' he flashed. 'If he won't give me the O.K. when I ask decently then I'll have her without it. There's more than one way of arranging a wedding.'

And that's exactly what he did. And, when she'd started the baby, of course they had to give in, but only her aunt attended the wedding.

Ironically, soon afterwards, Turton was commissioned and posted on an admin course and Caroline miscarried. But, whether that put things right with the uncle I don't know.

That wrapped the business up and neither of us saw her again because we were posted two hundred miles off into Devon, on a trade course, to be turned into photographers, a week before the wedding. We had a day's notice, that's all, so quick that I didn't even have time to let Mr. Ridd know that I wouldn't be able to play the next Saturday and I felt badly about it as I hate letting folks down.

But we should have stayed at Budmouth and been content to collect salvage because three months later the entire course was posted overseas. No-one had known it to happen before. That's how we came to be at Blackfen. And, once there on the shores of the good old Ship Canal, Budmouth, cricket, Caroline, became a dream, something you scarcely could be sure had ever happened.

Two

Well, that was old history. Now it was Blackfen and the Boat and the crawling weeks. And, naturally, rain.

Some erks, believing like my grandad that yea, even at the gaping mouth of Hell there is an entrance to Heaven, remustered for training on the longest courses they could root up in the Air Forces Manual. In fact, there was an encouraging tale of a rigger (somebody even knew his exact number) who had done this and no sooner arrived on India's coral strand, with a certain expectation of frying for five years, than he was whisked off to the Orderly Room and told to pack his bags because a posting to an instrument basher's course at Shepton Mallett had beaten him out there. And when this lazarus reached U.K. again, they immediately found his poor brain couldn't cope, so he was shot off to a dummy flarepath on the Cornish Riviera where he was billeted on a lush hotel and lived in sun and sin with the landlord's (absent in India, of course) wife and daughter, who took it turn and turn about to serve him in bed with breakfast and full b-bawd (as Wakerly put it).

So we applied for a course in radio-mechanics (six months). Not that I personally had any real faith in the story—though it was a good and inspiring one. My belief was that, like performing dogs, the Blackfen clerks were trained to smile and hand out forms and smile and smile and file them in In-trays with false bottoms joined up with a chute to the incinerator. Let's face it, when the finger was on you, Blackfen *was* the Boat.

You might sneer but all but a blind man could see that

there was a System: chaps kept disappearing. It was sinister if you dared think about it. Sometimes, you'd come to with a start and ask yourself, 'Where's so-and-so, the bloke with those red poplin pyjamas, the one who lived over there where that stranger's laid out?'

I've mentioned it before that to be around at midnight was a Must. This was when the Alarms went off once each week, and every hut was turned inside out and doubled off by the gestapo to a hangar, a high, empty place, as vast as York Minster, where blue lamps shed a deathbed look. Then, the same voice you hear announcing late trains began bashing out lists of names and numbers . . . 394 A.C.I. Smith J. L. . . . 002 L.A.C. Jones N. C. . . . 685 Corporal McLaren R. W. . . . and when the poor devil heard himself so described, he had to step out one pace, stamp his boots and bawl a despairing 'Sir' at the microphone This experience so shook him off balance, that, there and then, he began to gibber about his eleven good reasons for remaining in the U.K. But it was useless as hammering at a coffin lid; he was on the Boat and we only wanted to forget that we ever knew him. And twenty-four hours later he wasn't there any more and there were eleven more poor folk to wrestle as best they could with the Poor Law Guardians. Their prop and pillar had entered another World, as you might say.

Sometimes, whole huts were emptied as though by plague. If you looked in through the door there'd be abandoned kit, pullovers, mufflers loving hands had knit, sometimes even a pair of boots or a civvy suit they'd made some poor wretch disgorge. I remember making myself go on the scrounge because of clothes-rationing, and I found three cardigans and the pair of mittens I still use in winter. The other stuff I sent back to Grandad—clothes wear out fast on a farm.

But Wakerly's and my name were never called. He said that he knew a clerk up at Records and that he'd written to this man to scratch our two names from the registers with

31

a razor blade so that, now, we didn't really exist any more outside Blackfen and, so long as we kept our counsel, we could stay here till the War was over. All we had to do was never be first or last in queues, never laugh or look sour and, as far as exp-pedient, converse only with each other. In fact to think *p-permanently* and look like Lancasheer scenery. So I joined Boots Library and he joined a church choir (which he said would be good for his stammer). The great pity was, it being winter their cricket clubs were closed, because, whatever else you might think about Lancasheer, they understand the game—up to a point.

But it was a deadly time—the planlessness got me down. I don't want to harp on it but I'm the sort who looks a long way ahead, often as much as four or five years. You always get what you want—or so I believed then—provided you decide early what it is you *do* want. After that, it's all a matter of nudging the old boat in roughly the right direction and let her go with the current. That was the way I found best suited me because by nature I'm secretive and, to quote the Bible, tend to pursue my ends deviously.

Wakerly knew only one kind of life—where the virtues of Education were dinned into you, how it got you the right school, the right passes in the right subjects, then the right job at the right salary (with a pension). He never really understood that each class has its own way of living which it knows is best. It was no use even trying to tell him that, once I got back to The Vale after this, ten thousand a year wouldn't shift me or that all I wanted was to have a place of my own, be well thought of and not be imposed upon by anyone, big or little. And perhaps, in my wildest dreams, to play two or three games for the County 2nd Team. But back of all and above all—to be independent. [My mother had this on the brain.]

My grandad owned two hundred and thirty acre, fairish arable land; his landlord had made him buy it after the first war. He was well enough off to have sent me to St. Peter's, York, let alone a grammar school. But he'd left school when he was twelve and told me I was lucky to stay on till I was fourteen. That was the way he saw it, and he wasn't the sort you could discuss things with. Once he'd made up his mind, you either liked it or lumped it. Looking back, living with him was an education in itself.

I sometimes wondered what Wakerly would have said— or Caroline Driffield—if he could have seen us at it. We used to have our breakfast at a long, scrubbed table in the Room (as he called it), which had a stone slabbed floor, nobody talking because meals were for no purpose but eating. Then one of my sisters went to fetch the Bible from the Front Room, only used on Sundays, and Grandad read the passage for the day. He never told us how he picked, but it was supposed to be a direct communication from God. He used to begin with a groan, 'O Thou who knowest our secret imaginings . . . (this used to shake me when I was about seventeen and wrestling with the first onslaught of Sex) . . . let some portion of Thy Word fall upon some sinful heart here present . . .' Always that; that's why I remember. Then, when that was over, we'd push back our chairs and down we'd go on the stone. Wesleyans don't read prayers: they invent them as they go along or, as they claim, the spirit moves them. Grandad used to petition the Almighty with plenty of 'thees' and 'thous' as though he was an eastern potentate who happened to be a not too distant relative. He was a steady pray-er, a bit on the humdrum side maybe: he'd take a couple of minutes to pray himself in, then he'd consolidate. But he lacked style.

Once he moved into top gear, droning steadily on, there was nothing you could do except kneel it out and I used to study a yellow schoolroom map of The World, printed on shiny oil-cloth and hanging from a roller. Having good eyesight, that's where I first became acquainted with West

Africa—but this map was so out of date that it had Slave Coast, Ivory Coast, Grain Coast as well as Gold Coast instead of Sierra Leone, Ghana, Nigeria etcetera. I don't want to go on about this. But it has to do with the story because, without it, you can't really understand what I did. Things are either black or white to dyed-in-the-wool Wesleyans like our family was. It was rooted in us and that, in part, was to blame for what happened at Sinji. There was God and there was the Devil. Things were Right or Wrong, no In-between.

But I never talked about this to Wakerly because, though I knew he was too well brought-up to laugh, he couldn't be expected to believe that, even before I was eighteen, I'd been 'saved' twice by touring evangelists. This wears you down and, if you bother to work it out, explains quite a number of things that happened on the Coast. Anybody who's been through a couple of those revivalist weeks, fighting like mad to stop yourself from going under in the shameful way they made you, losing dignity and self respect and, in the end, beaten down as they 'sang you Home' (the final, sickening defeat)—anybody who's been through that is slightly bent for keeps.

As I said before, at Blackfen it was the past we thought about: nothing else made sense. There was the radio and there was the rain, and we sprawled on our pits tuned in to one or the other. Some chaps used to read but only the *Mirror* or some ghastly sex-soaked catalogue of undressing, peeping, petting, copulating. And anything really awful rated a public rendering. I particularly remember one so I must have listened to it too. 'Flora' or 'Flaming Flesh'—all about a French girl who started promisingly at eight by being pursued on tiptoe by decaying men who peeped through the keyhole when she 'left the room' during Saturday morning ballet classes and went on to fulfil her early promise between then and eighteen: *everything* happened to poor Flora. It was revolting.

I remember Wakerly coming in from his flooded tent during one of these recitals of pop minstrelsy. He was appalled. 'It's n-not the filth, Tom, I deplore,' he said, 'it's j-just the low literary standard. You mustn't be content with this muck. Your tragedy was not going to grammar school. Your education had scarcely s-started when they stopped it.' Then he drew up a reading list in case we were separated when our turn came. I came across it the other day: only the first two books were ticked off. I stuck at *Tristram Shandy*, even though a North Riding man wrote it.

When it got round to December and the Midnight Call still hadn't sounded, we joined an evening institute and enrolled in an art class because we thought the girl students would be more free and easy there than say the secretarial ones. The man lent us a paint-box and got us drawing a stuffed bird. At that time, I thought it was a vulture. Looking back, I can't think this teacher *wanted* us in his class; perhaps he tolerated us because he felt guilty that he wasn't called up himself. Wakerly turned out to be talented and the man praised him quite a bit so that he began to talk about not going back to the prep school where he used to teach and said we ought to emigrate to the South Seas after the War and live in a hut of palm leaves. Personally I didn't get much out of the class. There was only one girl student and she was rather common. But I kept going every Monday and Thursday; it made me feel permanent. And I went because Wakerly went.

But, in the end, it happened to me. The Midnight Peal sounded and the cry, 'To the hangars!', the blue lights and the raffle draw. Then I heard mine—'1293393 Flanders T.' and I couldn't believe it. I felt stunned. The names went on and then the lucky ones swarmed off and left us, the ones the finger was on, scores of us. They read us the Riot Act— 'No-one to leave camp again, No-one to write any letters, No phone-calls cancelling dates . . .'

We trudged back to the billets and threw ourselves on the beds. The others turned their backs and pulled blankets over their heads as we'd done so many times before. No-one wanted to know us now we were for the mincing machine. Next day I packed up my spare cap-badge and my RAF pint mug (for my mother's china cabinet in case I didn't make the return journey) and put all my spare cash, about twenty pounds, into an envelope, asking them to bank it for me. Then I wrote a few lines about being in God's hands for Grandad's sake and Everything being for the best for my mother—neither of which I believed. Then I gave her a few instructions such as getting somebody to keep the tyres of my motor-bike blown up and to see its engine was turned-over every couple of months and reminded her to wipe my two bats in the loft with linseed oil. And so on. Not having a girl friend certainly simplified matters.

That day shot past and at ten at night we had to parade in the full webbing I'd been carting around for a couple of years in a suit case: I'd never tried to fasten it together, let alone wear it. But I got into it after a fashion. The man who invented it can never have tried wearing it. In fact it was said that it wasn't a man but was Lady Astor, an M.P., who'd thought it up 'to keep their minds off sex'—the poor woman wrongly got the blame for no end of things such as the stuff they put into our tea whenever we went on Seven Days (to prevent us raping First Class passengers) and the yellow armlets all men returning from Overseas were said to wear to show they most likely had V.D.

Truthfully, that march to the Blackfen Railway Station in the pitch dark was about the worst thing that happened to me in the War. About two miles stumbling through blackness and this webbing grinding into my neck. Even when we got there, they wouldn't let us take it off and the justice of this must be admitted because we'd never have got it on again. Naturally, they'd got us there an hour too early.

At last the train crept in. Not a light on it. They prised us into it like a consignment of bullocks. We more or less lay where we fell, entangled in our own kit. No wonder they hadn't persecuted us much at Blackfen if they knew this was going to happen to us: they must have hooted when they saw we thought we were getting away with things. Then I heard a familiar voice groaning below me. It was Wakerly. For almost a day I'd been so full of my own misery I'd completely forgotten him. So we picked and wrestled each other's burdens from our backs and fell into the deep, contorted sleep of wartime travellers. No-one knew where we were going and no-one cared. Now and then I awoke and heard the wheels rocking along at top speed. Once we stopped and I heard voices calling below us in foreign language; I worked out later that we must have paused near Newport. Eventually daylight came, and the train stopped and didn't move again. It was very cold and we were by the sea; you could smell it. I peered out. It was still raining of course, and we were surrounded by derricks and cranes. A few gloomy railway men and dockers were staring up from the pools and puddles. Beyond them I could see a scatter of lifeless, sea-coloured ships.

'This is it,' Wakerly said. 'We're there, but it's taken them a couple of years to get us there.'

'Where's "there"?' I asked.

'On the edge of the War,' he said.

They shovelled us into the nearest boat, quite a sizeable job, a converted one-funnel cargo steamer called the *Mungo Park* and, once up the gangway and down four flights of temporary stairway into what had been the hold, even the craziest optimist knew that the story about the man who escaped from India to breakfast in bed with the landlord's daughter was a lie, and that he personally was not going to see his Native Land for a very long time.

Three

We sailed off down the Bristol Channel that same afternoon. Everybody crowded the rails to see the last of U.K. There was an educated airman from Tunbridge Wells standing next to me; he looked and sounded like an officer. He was very neat and had a clipped moustache. He was very informative and pointed out the islands as we passed them, Flathom, Moorholm, Lundy and told me about the birdwatching he'd done on them. This kind of life being bossed around by boneheaded regulars must have been gall and wormwood to him, used as he was to his independence and with a wife and a few inferiors trembling for their jobs, to vent his spleen on when his digestion was out of order or he wasn't being buttered up enough.

But we'd no more seen the last of England than my fanny. First we hung about Milford Haven and then we rolled along the Welsh coast and round the top corner where the mountains are, miles of them, into Liverpool Bay. Other ships tagged on and, when we were near the port itself, a couple of naval vessels, corvettes, I think, showed up overnight.

'They're escorting us back to Blackfen,' Wakerly said. 'Tomorrow we'll be steaming east up the Ship Canal . . . dressed overall.'

'And anchor in the tent compound,' I said.

'And when they've unveiled a tablet over your billet-door —FLANDERS WAS HERE—we're all going to be demobbed and sent to lecture to overseas drafts on Our Experiences, to delude them into cherishing faith that there's still an escape hatch even when you're on the Boat. It's a clever gambit to bolster morale by the Top Brass just below Cabinet level.'

And he spread it around that this was going to happen and no end of erks believed it. It was truly amazing how dim most of that boatload were. Education seemed to have left no impression on them at all. I'd always believed England was the greatest country and that we were the finest nation the Earth had ever known but now I admit I began to wonder how we kept afloat with so many dimwits hanging round our necks.

Next day, even in my hammock, I knew there'd been a change. When I crawled up the four flights of temporary timber to the top, there was only sea and ships in sight, wallowing along west and Wakerly explained there'd been a change of plan and we'd been reprieved to service a lush basic-training station in California—('It'll be too expensive to send us back when we get out there. Palm trees, gorgeous starlets with violet eyes, b-beautiful brainless chicks hungry for men, no rationing, cream with everything . . .')

And, to give substance to his prophecy, a canteen opened up, selling fags a bob for twenty and as much milk chocolate as you could pay for. Immediately a queue started, dwarfing any line that ever inched round four sides of an Odeon on a rainy Saturday night and soon, men, delirious with greed, were stumbling down the temporary stairways clutching two or three dozen chocolate bars to their chests, their uniforms bulging with fags. And this went on till more men were sick from chocolate than from sea and it lay squashed into a fungoid kit-bag lining.

Meanwhile, the old *Mungo Park* bashed on through the grey Atlantic. Down in its belly everything creaked, and Wakerly said that the inner casing which kept out the water was working loose and would rip right off when we met the mountainous waves he'd read about in Joseph Conrad. Then

39

he went on to tell willing hearers that the old crate had only been passed safe for the flat waters of Lake Tchad (in the Dry Season) until the War came and human beings could be killed off freely by officials. ('It's to do with an internationally agreed de-population scheme: we're over-eating the world's food supply.')

They fed us lots of beans and dumplings and sterilized tea. In fact, there was no stint of food but as fast as you took it in you threw it back; this was because the M.P. rolled so much. This, said Wakerly, was because her rounded bottom was designed (originally) for coasting in the Persian Gulf—where it had sunk quietly once on the Grand Sandbar of Oman and had been serviced with a new bottom, what was left of the original bottom being now this same inner lining which was working loose.

They said that there was a complete flying-boat squadron aboard—except for the aircrew which would follow us out from Mount-Batten when we'd set up shop. But you couldn't tell how true this was because we were embedded in a crawling mob of enough soldiery to fight a second Zulu Campaign. Then it was spread around that we'd all be sorted out when we got to Florida. ('We've been switched from California by a cable from Lady Astor.'—Wakerly.)

But we woke up one morning going south.

'Definitely India,' Wakerly explained. 'Farewell Florida. But there are compensations—the natives will do anything for sixpence.'

We all spent our sixpences in different ways. The Mysterious East! Personally, I was quite pleased; I knew from Wisden that cricket was played there with fair skill even though only on matting wickets.

It was growing quite warm now for a normal November. This made the nights more horrible. When the beds were slung from the ceiling, you couldn't shift but by crawling. We were crammed in like lice under a stone. God knows what horrors would have taken place if we'd been torpedoed! They say one brave officer found his way down the four flights of stairs one night and stood on the threshold, eyes popping, his hand over his nose, repeating 'Incredible!' You have to remember that we were two decks below where even seamen would normally have slept.

The lavatories! Dim, half-explored regions with a hot, clarty stench which I tried to place. Stables? Cow byres? Half way down the Atlantic I got it. Rabbits! A warren of rabbits had just left! Now why would that be? The *Mungo Park* could never have humped a cargo of rabbits up the Gulf of Oman! Maybe rats but not rabbits. Well, these lavatories struck with terror even erks who came from Salford or Leeds, where one lavatory does for four families, or Mid-Wales (with its unbelievable arrangements up the orchard), even *they* lined the seats with book pages or they separated their persons from the diseased wood by supporting themselves on their hands and smoking in big puffs to cancel out rabbit.

Well, that was how we made out as we rolled imperially along to India, comforting ourselves that, slaves as we were now, we'd be princes there. At night, we used to sit around the same scrubbed tables where we ate. Some played cards and some wrote letters they couldn't post, instalments of the longest letters they'd ever write to their wives and sweethearts. Here, I felt out of it because card games bore me and, as I'd only my mother to write to (I couldn't even imagine writing to my grandad), there didn't seem much use upsetting her with an account of this floating Black Hole of Calcutta. Even short trips on stopping trains worried her; she'd never been out of Yorkshire. She'd never been out of the North Riding for that matter.

Then, from a conversation on deck in the dark with an officer, I found that it wasn't India after all. 'Soon we'll be swinging west,' he said. 'There's going to be a big push against Rommel, just as soon as the new general, Montgomery, gets these new squadrons. When the *Mungo Park* docks he'll swing into a massive attack and drive on through Greece, Bulgaria, Czecho-Slovakia and into the Soft Belly of Germany itself. We'll be home by Christmas.'

As you must have gathered, all important decisions about the War are taken at night (to stop you protesting against them). He was right except for one detail. Next morning the convoy had disappeared to further the great cause of Home by Xmas. But not us—we were jogging along alone. The sea now looked much bigger and the way to India dicier. They hadn't even left us a sloop.

'It's part of the international plot,' Wakerly said. 'They've decided to get rid of us to relieve the rationing and to keep the War going with the insurance on the *Mungo Park.*'

From then on, I decided the deck was the safest place and never lingered long in my hammock after waking. Climbing up next day to smell the real air, I found the sun still level with the sea and us going straight east towards it. The rumours now became fairly stable and settled on the West Coast of Africa. Bathurst, the Gambia, Sierra Leone, Accra, Takoradi, Lagos, Dakar were all spoken of knowledgeably. I'd heard of them but they were like Peterborough and Oswestry, places you know of from railway timetables but never get off at. The village schoolmaster, who'd learnt his geography in Victorian times, used to parcel the lot up as The White Man's Grave, a title which gave us a pleasant shudder. He made us repeat,

> 'Beware, O beware
> The Bight of Benin,
> Where few come out
> Though many go in.'

Meanwhile, the folklore of that region developed vigorously around the mess table. It was said that the great scorpions there changed colour to render themselves invisible before creeping in to kill with a sting from the tail aimed unerringly at the throat. And ants in armies which built tunnels secretly under billets so that roofs fell in and crushed you in your sleep. Besides these, there were day-to-day hazards such as swallowing screw-worms with your tea and these ate steadily through your testicles causing the same to wither until, one morning, you woke up singing soprano. It sounded an extraordinary place . . . mongooses (some said this was 'mongeese'), illuminated jelly-fishes and praying-mantises which were said to devour their partners whilst copulating. The women—professionals were kept in cages, but the amateurs roamed the paths wagging immense backsides and busts smelling of stale bacon: for half-a-dollar you were dragged off for an astonishing quarter-hour in the bush.

But Wakerly (I fancy he was upset by this non-fiction competition) said that this was all nonsense. He declared that White Man's Grave had been put out of business by white man's medicine, and that my schoolmaster's stories of traders changing looking-glasses for diamonds and elephant tusks had been invented by Rider Haggard. (I should have realised that he was unreliable as a gen-man from his captaincy of the village side on Saturdays: he thought the *only* way to beat the other side was for our batsmen to score more runs than their batsmen. Basic Cricket!)

In fact, I reckon the only man aboard who had any pukka gen was the officer-material soldier, the Birdman from Tunbridge Wells, who had told me of his tent holidays on Flatholm and Lundy, watching our feathered friends. He knew so much that I switched off whenever he began to reel off lists of birds he was looking forward to seeing—the ibis, the calliope humming-bird, the flamingo . . . His wife probably

43

was missing him in bed and the garden, but I bet she wasn't sorry to be having a break from birds.

The other spring of wisdom was a medical orderly known as Blubber, who looked like a dropsical Eskimo and who was a sex fiend. He was at the other end of the boredom scale— just vulgar. The Birdman and he just grated against each other—their birds were not of the same feather.

'I'll tell you about a bird,' this Blubber used to butt in with. 'A big blonde bird; she has a downy little love nest over a sweet-shop in Tottenham, black silk plumage down to the skin. Ten bob to perch half an hour with her, three quid for a night's roost.' Then he'd go into revolting detail of what she'd do to oblige a cock-bird as he used to put it. The bona-fide birdman had to sit through it in order to eat but used to try to block the sound by conversing with Wakerly, the only one of us who he acknowledged as his own species. This put Wakerly's back up—not being a snob himself. In fact, he may even have been annoyed at being blocked from giving his full attention to the sickening sex-life of blonde birds and black birds by the staider account of the Jamaica firetail's decent home-life. (Let's face it: he was never quite the same after Turton had taken Caroline Driffield. He let his standards go. He fought it but it beat him. Well, we all have our weaknesses.)

'Them black birds,' this awful man used to say (you had to listen or miss a meal) 'I've read about them in a book a pal lent me, a very rare book somebody rich lent *him*, a connoisseur (all the cheap editions are banned). They develop into fully-fledgeds at ten and that's when the black males initiate them. At ten they are taken to the witch-doctor in the middle of the bush, and he fastens them to the floor of his hut, and then he lights a little fire of tropical herbs which puts them in a state and they wave their legs in the air, moaning and begging somebody to be quick and do them. Then, when the witch doctor and the chief have had the first go, all the men and boys get a turn and then she's auctioned off to the highest bidder.'

'About how much do they ask, would you say?' a little man in gold rimmed spectacles asked—he'd told us he was a grocer and came from Wisbech. 'I'm only asking for information.'

'All depends on her measurements and her Nubility,' Blubber replied, dwelling lovingly on this last word. 'The blacks like fat women, good child bearers and hard workers. A black's ambition is to buy a fat woman who will work hard in bed and the back garden.'

'In fact, a w-winner Home and Away,' put in Wakerly.

'You can buy a real whizzer for a couple of cows. Widows are cheaper; maybe no more'n a couple of goats or pigs. But you have to remember that the brother-in-law gets first refusal, and he doesn't get charged anything.'

'How many can a man have?' asked the Wisbech grocer ('Only for information').

'As many as his strength and money can run to. Our missionaries are wasting their time out there, because when it comes to a choice of one God/one wife, and half a dozen gods/half a dozen wives, it goes without saying.'

As I looked around the table I thought a Moslem missionary would find it dead easy rustling up a dozen converts. Then, because I'd eaten enough and too much sex talk puts me off, I volunteered to collect the dirty plates and, after, I climbed up to the deck. Unfortunately the true Birdman caught me.

'So you find that kind of talk nauseating too, Flanders?" he began. 'I don't mind the Danger etc. of War; but having to mix with men like Blubber is a bit much. When we're settled on a station, I shall apply for a commission.'

Just then Wakerly came up, so I said would they excuse me as I had to write a letter. I knew his sort. I bet he'd been turned down for a commission three times already. All his kind seemed to think that going to a certain school and talk-ing in a certain way gave them a God-given Right to be an officer. Turton was just such another. At Budmouth you could see that he'd promoted himself in his imagination, like this one. But what could they *do*? That's how I judged people then. As my grandad used to say, 'By their works shall ye know them!' Well, it's true.

What was Tunbridge-Wells doing here, in heavy, stiff, black boots, a suit like a million others, parcelled up at night in a hammock, by day wedged on a bench with nine others, eight of whom he despised, taking his turn to carry up the slops?

Let's face it; he should never have been dragged away from his four-bedroomed detached in a quarter-acre of suburb, three nice children at a nice school, a nice maid per-suading him back to consciousness with a nice cup of tea in a nice bed with an adoring china-blue-eyed wife. The cellar of the *Mungo Park* was the place of Blubber and such as Blubber. And me, I suppose, being used to muck.

So I left him explaining birds to Wakerly who could take it smiling. In fact, he even may have enjoyed it because, next morning, 'It opened my eyes,' he said. 'I thought he was just another mess-bore like that sick-quarters ghoul. But he's a real gen-man. Sea-birds are his field. Do you know he spends all his summer holidays catching and ringing them. He has a wife and three children and they all go with him. They live in a tent on an island. He says the eldest girl, Phillipa, can identify two hundred and seventy species by sight and one in three by song. And she's only nine. Astonishing!'

I agreed that it was very impressive and took even more care to avoid him. I only hoped his wife and three clever children *liked* spending their holidays on a dull island sleep-ing on the ground, talking all day about birds. What kind of brains have birds! I mean what can they *do*? Is there any-

46

thing more stupid than a bird? Evidently this man had never had any intimate dealing with birds on the farm, getting one lot to lay eggs while you scared away another lot from devouring the pea fields. The only bird I saw any sign of sense in was a cockerel bullying a penful of fowls for his pleasure. If Wakerly saw it differently, well I suppose it was because *he* was different and looked at things differently. I've probably said it before, but he wasn't all that easy to understand. I expect there were folks like him on The Vale but they were the sort we didn't mix with. My grandad grouped them under the general heading of Parasites and, on Sundays, Abominations, chiefly because they came roaring in fast cars to The Lamb. It probably was a fair exchange of back-handers because I heard they called us 'the Coolies'.

I never was really sure why Wakerly palled up with me, though once I remember him saying, 'Tom, what I like about you is that you're your own man.' By this I expect he meant that I was independent. Well, that was true because I took after my mother who was East Riding (and, as is well known, they are different).

When I was a lad she drummed it into me, 'Be independent, Tom. Don't let anybody get you in his pocket. And one other thing—I'd rather you were brought home dead than drunk.' This two-pronged philosophy made a deep impression on me.

Four

All this time, the *Mungo Park* rolled along confidently. The sea was pretty level and the breeze warmer. As this particular afternoon turned suddenly to night, we noticed that a corvette had appeared from nowhere. 'It's because we're nearly there,' Wakerly said. 'It's been sent to bring us in. We'll be staining the beaches this time tomorrow. At Dakar.'

Half that shipload hadn't a clue where they were. It must have been frightening for them. They used to come and ask Wakerly. If you don't know where you are, Bridlington is as remote as Lourenco Marques and that sounds about as far as they could post you. (It was the name painted on the galvanized iron basin I used to shave in every morning I spent on that Coast.)—'Lourenco Marques' . . . I still don't know where it is and why that particular basin never reached there.

They were right about one thing as it turned out. West Africa. When I climbed up to the deck a sailor told me. 'It's all right to tell you now,' he said. 'We're clear of the U-boat Zone.'

When Wakerly came up, I told him and we got out of the heat round a corner. The sun was low. In these latitudes it grew dark as soon as it sank. By this time he'd changed his tune.

'That bird-fanatic caught me and has been binding on like the clappers ever since—"You're the only one I feel who's on my wave-length, Wakerly . . ." '

'What's today's Talk about?' I asked, 'The purple-breasted boola-boola?'

'No, his wife. Big strapping farmer's girl. ("A gentleman farmer's daughter.") He trapped her when she was eighteen. His sort are cunning, hard as nails when they smell out something they want for their comfort. He kept binding on about her being not too bright but how wonderful she was in bed. "She's so good for me" he kept saying as though she was a bottle of medicine. And now he's no-one's little tin-pot god, he's in purgatory. I bet he'd invite Hitler in tomorrow so long as he'd let him get back to her bed and his birds.'

Like Turton, I thought. And Caroline—he caught *her* young too. I didn't need to say this aloud because I knew Wakerly was thinking the same.

We set off downstairs. He stopped on the deck above ours. 'God,' he said, 'it's bedlam down there. I'm going to sleep on deck tonight. It smells worse than usual—*sick* rabbits now. And listen.'

The whole mess-deck was shouting Nellie Dean, a vast hopeless roaring of men without women, men who'd lost their footholds. Even Blubber must have had some place, I thought, where even *he* was Somebody.

> 'And the waters as they flow' they roared,
> 'Seem to whisper soft and low,
> "You're my heart's delight;
> I *love* you Nellie Dean." '

'They're crying for their pubs and clubs, their factories and chapels and all their back-street family albums of girl-friends and wives under bushes and on beds, the whole lot g-gilt with glamour it n-never had and never can have,' Wakerly said. 'Read it up in my Social History of the War, Vol. IV, published 1984.'

'Well, be fair,' I said, 'they don't know where they're going or what's going on or what's going to happen to them.

What else is there for them to shout for except what's past? Don't you ever think about it yourself?'

He didn't speak for a couple of minutes. 'Yes,' he said, 'I do—sometimes. No, often . . .

"Before it is too late, before we forget
The cherries white in the woods and the curdled clouds
And the lapwing crying low above the plough . . ."

Remember?'

He said it quietly.

I could have kicked myself almost as soon as I'd asked him.

'Don't you ever think back to things and wish you could have time over again, Tom?' He asked quickly, but not turning his head.

'No,' I said, 'I don't. Thank God!' And we went upstairs again.

It was a hot, breathless night, the sky bright with stars. Except for the rush of water there was no sound on the decks. The rails were lined with silent men. Others lay crooked on the hatches. And when it was too dark to see anymore, Wakerly went off to find a place on the boat-deck (though it was out of bounds to Other Ranks) and I went downstairs to my hammock.

The rest were still at it. No-one any longer seemed to care where he was going and the talk had gone back to the good old stand-bys—Sex and How much longer the War could last.

Blubber was still drilling away at his scabby view of booze and bed, and the rest were still dribbling and nodding, listening as unctuously as if he was expounding the Great Universal Secret of Life, Death and The World to Come.

'And I said to her, "You're not to go out of a night on the beer with men while I'm gone. I haven't got nothing to give you only my name. I have no Riches and Wealth to leave you in Luxury with, but I say this wiv my hand on my heart—if you go out with one bloody civvy, don't expect to get away wiv it because I'll break every stick of furniture and I'll thrash and batter you within one half-inch of your life and then I'll sling my hook and you'll never set eyes on me again no more." '

He was still hard at it when I fell asleep but the last thing I remember thinking was So Wakerly hasn't forgotten, he *hasn't* got over it, he *still* loves her.

Down at the bottom of the *Mungo Park* you couldn't tell what time it was; there were ceiling lamps burning all night. So I used to guess when it was dawn. On a farm you've no difficulty getting up and, next morning, as usual, I was the first. I bundled up the hammock, got into my slacks and tunic and made for the staircase, wondering if we'd changed direction back to California during the night. Half the hold was lost in shadows, odd limbs sticking out, someone groaning in a dream, faces rising to the surface in pools of light —Blubber the Worker sweating and snoring, and Birdman still looking put out in a Middle Class manner because he wasn't in his detached double-bed kicking out his madam to kick the maid into brewing up and serving him tea and the *Daily Telegraph* on a tray.

I began to climb the staircase, and I think I was toiling up the third stage when the torpedo hit us. All I remember was an almighty crash and the *Mungo Park* coming to a shuddering stop as though drawing in a great breath. I shot forward, then sideways, and then began to roll back down, grabbing at air until I snatched hold of a post. It was just as well I did, because the next drop would have taken me where I'd come from. I was in a panic. I could hear them shouting down below me but I didn't look. Not then. (I did later.) I set off smartly up to back where I'd been. And reached there just as the second torpedo hit. So down I slid again. It was like those games you play with flies when they're trying to crawl up a window-pane. It was murder. I suppose I shrieked with terror at my helplessness as I went rolling down only to catch a hold again at just about the same spot. As I hung there another bod came sliding down like a sledge. I remember thinking how odd he looked seeing him wrong way round. Because his hands were pointing upwards he couldn't get a grip on anything. Instinctively I shoved my legs through the bannisters and blocked the stairs. He ploughed head first into me.

'Up!' I yelled at him, 'Up!'

'Up!' I shouted again, and kneed him in the back. He turned his mad blue eyes at me like a dying duck. 'Thanks,' he said, and lunged upwards.

I must have been upside down myself because I saw a mob below me and I recall thinking, They'll tread me under; I'm finished. They looked crazy, eyes popping, mouths gaping, all still in their shirts. And shrieking. I seemed to be moving upwards. Then I saw it was the other way round—*they* were falling as their stretch of staircase gave way to crash like a rush of logs over a waterfall, leaving me at the edge of the pit, the catastrophe twisting like a film running wild off the sprockets.

Above, I could see bods bashing their way up and out of it, and I tried to drag myself after them and wondered why I couldn't. And only then I saw the hands pinning my right arm against the last step. More talons than fingers, they gripped so fiercely. I twisted my head: it was the Birdman, his agonized face swayed below me, no more than two feet from my own.

'Off! off!' I shouted and would have struck him, only that I was holding on with my free hand.

'Off!'

There was but one thing to do. I forced the arm he was gripping off the step and, immediately, his weight dragged it vertically downwards so that his own hands slid along it.

His nails scraped grooves of skin from the back of my hand and then he fell and I was free. So I picked myself up and scuttled up the staircase like an animal, grunting with fear. I got off the contraption just as it swung out too far, twisted, and went crashing down too on top of the poor devils trapped at the bottom.

The startling thing was that, after the nightmare, it was broad daylight up on top. But the shambles! Men were pushing in all directions and yelling their heads off. It was like being squeezed out of a football ground. (And all the time there was this awful muffled screaming coming from back down the hole.) Some of the davits wouldn't work and someone was shouting that boats from the First Class decks were getting away half empty so there was a dash in that direction. A young army lieutenant had pulled out a re-volver and managed to get his men into ranks and one bosun got a boat lowered from the upper deck to them. Two or three chaps near me had dragged a raft to the side and tipped it over and jumped after it. I slipped amongst the soldiers but their officer yelled, 'Get out of it, you bloody air-job!' and waved his weapon.

The old *Mungo Park* gave a massive heave. That *really* scared me, but I could still see the men with the raft. One bloke waved up at me and was shouting something ('Jump' I suppose) so I climbed on the rail, held my nose and dropped. I couldn't swim and hoped for the best. Actually there was so much stuff in the water that you couldn't miss. I went under and came up clawing, and then someone got hold of me and, between us, I got on the raft. One soldier was screaming, 'Paddle her off with your hands or we'll be sucked in when she goes under.' I don't know if there was any truth in it, but getting away from the side made sense, be-cause a lifeboat above us full of men was jerking about on its davits and couldn't be lowered. Then the old *Mungo Park* gave an almighty lurch, and down this boat crashed non-stop on top of another one just pulling away. You could hear the ghastly crunch. I couldn't look. I just hope it killed most of them straight off.

I won't labour things: once they were afloat again, the naval blokes got a grip on themselves and began giving orders and rounding up rafts and swimmers and hauled us away. Then we watched the M.P. settling in the water. Nobody spoke and we sat listening in horror to them shrieking back in the hold. Except it wasn't so loud in the distance. I thought of the Birdman and hoped the falling staircase had killed him. As far as that goes, Blubber too, and I wondered what happened to their wives and if they would forget and take up with other men.

When she finally went, she went with a rush. Afterwards, I found out that from the first torpedo to her sinking had only been six minutes.

The corvette was racing around like mad pumping out depth charges which were going off like muffled guns and sending up water-spouts, but after a time it calmed down and put out nets for us to climb up. It took an hour or two before what were left of us were aboard and then she began to move very fast, swerving towards the land. All this evidently had happened not too far outside a harbour. The sea was like glass and soon we saw a low bank of land, wooded, and perhaps hills or clouds farther back still. As we got into the estuary it was night again and, when they got us ashore, we couldn't see much though there wasn't a blackout. In fact, if it hadn't been for the peculiar rotten sort of smell you wouldn't have known where you were. If you were to ask me what the West Coast of Africa basically is like . . . you know, like stone being heavy and water wet—I'd answer, Africa is hot, black and smells. By day the one, at night, the other. Really black. And from this blackness you can always hear voices and smell this smell. And so it was now. We huddled at the quayside and stared into the darkness, trying to take it all in. Many people were there, looking at us, giggling, whispering. But we couldn't see them.

I'll tell you an odd thing. Up to this moment, I'd never thought about Wakerly nor what had happened to him. I was too stunned by what had happened to *me*. Then, sitting there in the darkness, I thought, *Wakerly! Did he make it?* And I got up stiffly and began to look around for him.

Five

I found him standing under a lamp no more than a few yards distant, looking blank.

I said, 'Are you O.K.?'

He looked up and I could see he'd forgotten me as I'd forgotten him. They say that Yorkshiremen are sparing of words. That's a laugh. If anything, they're over-given to them. And they talk wildly and too big. It's the Londoner, especially the suburban variety, that latches his mouth in a crisis: put my back to a Londoner's any time when the heat's on. I couldn't have borne it to have had Wakerly wringing my hand and dripping on me. And, of course, he didn't. He just burst out laughing. And, then, so did I.

' "POOR GETTERS-UP ARE EARNESTLY ADVISED TO SLEEP ON THE ROOF-TOP" ' he said.

'The stairs gave way,' I said, 'but I made it—just.' (I still could see Blubber upside down. And as for the other one. . . .)

He looked around. 'Well, at l-least we know where our tickets were made out for on this Mystery Cruise Guaranteed Packed with Thrills!'

For once, they didn't leave us hanging around. We were packed into some launches and told we were going down the River to our station, Sinji. 'Going down the River' . . . 'Sinji' . . . Romantic like a bit of H. Rider Haggard! And, really, it was—chugging along through the warm night and just a murmur of talking, after the day's hammering.

I could tell we were there when we passed a couple of red lights bobbing on the water marking the limit of the Trot and, soon, there were the shapes of a couple of Sunderlands stirring at their moorings. Even on the water (which reflects what light there is) it was pretty black, but you can't mistake a Sunderland: it's like no other kite. They really look like flying-boats, whereas the Catalinas we were to see so much of look like converted aeroplanes.

We turned into a kind of bay bounded by what looked like mangroves and saw the lights of a few buildings and the flash of transport head-lights changing direction, hidden now and then behind bends in a road, dipping and climbing amongst the slopes. I feel I ought to say I felt a thrill. I didn't, but I could tell from Wakerly's voice that he was excited. Africa meant nothing to me then. I knew nothing about it (except the out-of-date gen churned out by our village schoolmaster and the cock Blubber had invented), and I didn't want to know anything. Frankly, even after a year there, only its size made any real impression on me and that was how I remembered it—going on and on to the horizon and, beyond that, a thousand more miles and more to the next sea over on the other side. Too big, too much of it to understand, too many people, a great, lost land. It wasn't exciting. The opposite—depressing.

We nudged along a jetty, a wooden affair. Somewhere above us, a man shone an electric torch, looking us over I suppose, probably listening for groans like the movies (having heard of the *Mungo Park* thing).

'Mind near the top,' this man kept saying in a despairing voice. 'There's a rung missing . . . near the top. I keep reporting it. Don't blame me.'

'Oh, put the bung in it, Pinkney,' someone yelled from the boat. 'And take your finger out and give these lads a light . . .'

I crawled up the ladder and floundered over the edge, clutching at nothing, then gingerly rose as the man steadied me. 'Thanks,' I said. 'O.K.' he said, 'but don't turn or you'll be back into the mud over on the other side.'

A light from the launch lit his face for a moment. Pale, slightly constipated look, bulging eyes: this was Pinkney—for the next twelve months I slept opposite him. I stared at him and he at me. But that was the last time we spoke to each other.

There was a storm-lantern burning on a post. In that blackness, it just about lit itself, nothing else. It was like the end of the world—this jetty sticking out from Africa. I thought 'Well, I'm here. But what am I doing here? I mean what am I *really* doing here?'

No-one said much: we'd had enough for one day. Oddly enough—God knows why—I remembered what my mother used to make me repeat as I knelt by my bed on the flowery linoleum when I was a kid:

> 'For the Blessing of this day
> Thank you, God, I humbly pray.
> Make me steadfast, pure and bright.
> Keep me safe till morning light.'

She was a very practical woman but hadn't too much sense of humour. When Grandad said it was the Lord who'd saved me from the deep she added, '. . . And the training we gave him, getting up early . . .'

We were sent stumbling off up a gravel track, too tired to take in the place we'd been travelling so long and disastrously to reach. An N.C.O. shone a torch at a pile of folding beds and told us to take one ('You can have two if yer can hump 'em.') and kip in some tents he swore we'd find pitched beyond him in the blackness. No food, no lights, no explanation—the usual RAF low level bungle.

'W-what about the mosquito nets, Sergeant?' Wakerly asked. 'Shouldn't we have one?'

'They don't eat sprogs; yer smell of U.K.' he replied. And

he was right, we did. Even the salt water hadn't wiped off the taint of that old floating rabbit warren.

Well, he left us blundering over guy ropes and tent pegs, struggling to hide from the night, hoping we shouldn't dream of the day. Wakerly and I were separated and I fell over a bed frame and into a tent. Naturally, there was a bed there already. So just as you'd expect in the RAF, I had two bed frames and no mattress, so it was like lying on a harp, assisting the night's concert outside. And that's another thing about Africa: it's never still. There's always bumping and rustling, birds screaming, and the stir of millions of insects groping around. And feet. Feet padding softly past. The blacks sleep in shifts; they don't keep regular hours like us, so there's always someone stirring and watching. It became an obsession with me the longer I stayed there. Everybody had obsessions before they left The Coast. Even the biggest clods began to do crazy things like drawing birds in the sand and the ones with better educations usually cracked completely, and began feeding them. My two obsessions were the sound of feet running, and all the places that went on and on east of us, beyond the tropic rain forests on the other side of the mountains, right across the dry lakes and the deserts to Addis Ababa, Kilimanjaro and Zanzibar, all full of people who slept in shifts stirring and watching and running around in the blackness.

It was hot when I woke up next morning. I was lying on my back on the bare wires and there was an ugly great creature hanging upside down above me on the ridge pole, glaring down at me. Too big for an insect, too small for an animal. It had a long sharp tail, squat legs and a vile face. We stared at each other deciding who should spring at who first. I waved an arm but it didn't even flick its eyes let alone shift. I gave in, rolled out of bed on the opposite side to this Welcome to Africa delegation and left. Later I saw its picture in a book and it was a scorpion and it's supposed to take only one nip to kill. The odd thing was that for the rest of the time on The Coast I didn't see another.

Now, I saw that these tents were pitched amongst palm trees and that Sinji wasn't too bad a spot; much better than either Blackfen or the *Mungo Park*. A man told me where I could get some chop (I might as well begin using the local language), and I took my irons and went off to Liberian green coffee, biscuits mushed in milk from canned powder, a split, thin sausage and half a fried yam. Then a hard biscuit and either jam or pickle to smear over it. I used to take service food and cooking fatalistically . . . what they put up, that I ate; you have to live. Most of the erks wouldn't drink Liberian green coffee; they had tea on the brain, any sort of slosh so long as it looked like tea. The English lower classes are more conservative than the aristocracy in my opinion. If their mams had never given them whatever they found on their plates, they didn't even try it. 'What's this bloody muck!' was their usual reaction. They'd have said it about caviare or truffles. In fact, the very ones you'd think would eat whatever was poured into their troughs, ones who'd had a year or two on the Dole, were the most finicky. If they'd had their way, they'd have had cod and chips dowsed in Tiger Sauce three times a day. Just to give an illustration: right in the middle of the Working Area at Sinji was a mango tree, a very fine tree too like our walnut tree at home (the one with the grindstone below), its leaves so dense that it was as dark as looking up into the cellar. And it had a heavy crop of fruit, the sort of lush rarity you pay a half dollar apiece for if you live near Harrogate, Guildford or Tunbridge Wells (only such places stock mangos). And yet I bet Wakerly and I were the only ones who ever ate them. I'll admit it was Wakerly who got me to try them. But no-one else did; yet all you had to do was to stand on a chair and grab. I got to like them and, whilst they were in season, I always ate one for my morning break: they did a lot for

60

my sanitary habits in the early days when others were getting constipated.

I suppose I should give you a description of RAF Sinji, even though I never saw a map of it. (Though I take it there was one somewhere or they scarcely could have built a camp.) To the end of my time there, I never was sure where we stood in relation to the town and the other places in the colony which I heard of later as cricket fixtures. Of course, having come that way, I knew that the Atlantic was just up the River westwards and that, on each side of this same River, there was a plain where they grew monkey nuts for making margarine. Heaven knows where this River came from. I saw it from aircraft, of course. It crawled back eastwards across a baked plain, its banks punctuated with log jetties and makeshift quays and dumps of nuts waiting for the mini-steamer that chugged up and down it, making a round trip once a fortnight.

So I never got a clear picture in my mind of Sinji. It had no mountains like Sierra Leone. As far as I could tell, it was a mixture of silted-up mud, swamp and sand-hills; tropical marginal land the NFU would have called it, with its tip pushed into a very wide backwater (also edged by mangroves) and this backwater joined another one where was situated the Trot where the kites took off and landed. Except for the navigators, I don't think anyone, officers or erks, really knew where we were. Sinji was just a name, a place to live and, now and then, engine spares, letters and bodies reached there from the UK. Otherwise it ran to type like all wartime stations. It was like RAF Manston, RAF Bircham Newton, RAF Anywhere . . . a guard room, orderly room, cookhouse . . . I won't go on. It was just another big government fitting, like a pillar box or an employment exchange, and you knew immediately what it was and, more or less exactly where everything could be found, as soon as you

61

saw it. They all look near enough the same wherever you find them. The only difference at Sinji was that it was hotter.

The worst thing about it was that, whereas at RAF Cardington or RAF Church Fenton, you could escape from it to the civvy confusion of Bedford or Leeds, at RAF Sinji there was *nowhere* to go either for an evening out or for a forty-eight. No shops (well not what we call a shop, something with a cash register, a counter, show cases and full shelves), no cafes, no pubs. This is important because I don't want you to think of Sinji as being in Beau Gesteland with dancing girls and opium dens round the corner. At Sinji there was Nothing.

If you really want to know, Sinji was like three beads strung along a gravel road—the Billets—the Working Area —the Apron. This road ended on the Apron and there you took the launches to reach the kites. We only went down there when we had to. It was another world. Day in day out, before dawn, two or three flying-boats roared off into the air, disappearing away out over the South Atlantic. But, except as machines to service and fettle up with cameras and what not, we had no part of them and didn't want one. Or so we liked to think: *they* had to do with the War.

There was a jetty, as I've said, down there and it had a kind of guard's van at its terminus. It served as a shelter from the sun and, in the Wet Season, the downpour. We had to hang around there a lot, because there wasn't always a dinghy ready to take us out to work at the moorings. Maybe, it would be a better description if I said it was like a bus-shelter, because it was a hit-and-miss business like waiting for the market-day bus out on the moors at home. We had plenty of time to admire the view—millions of little crabs crawling in and out of the sand, and empty oil drums, red ones, lying around the beach like stranded sea-creatures. Now and then they were rounded up, taken into deep water and sunk but, more often than not, the blacks hammered them flat and used them as walls and roofs instead of mud and reeds. You don't need to get Planning Permission in Africa.

Well, that was RAF Sinji. Just one of hundreds of fitments all over Africa and Asia where thousands of protesting erks were enduring their first foreign holiday, dumped there to put down the Nazi Tyranny and raise Freedom's Banner high (as Wakerly said).

RAF Sinji! Sometimes I look around our chapel at Foreign Mission Festivals and watch people's faces bellowing, 'Where Afric's sunny fountains roll down the golden strand'—and have a quiet laugh.

Six

They kept us in tents for two more nights. No mosquito nets, no lamps, but I did find a mattress and a blanket. Wakerly told me they hadn't expected us for another fortnight; the usual RAF balls-up. It's only fair to say that RAF orderly-rooms were so over-staffed with so little to do that they fought the war on two fronts, one as urged by Mr. Churchill and the *Daily Express*, and the other (pursued with real energy and venom) as laid down by the Air Ministry Manual of Correct Procedure. And, after the War, they dispersed to Whitehalls and town halls, their skills of authorised bloody-mindedness beautifully perfected, to persecute, disorganise and delay.

At Sinji, they built up a really efficient little army of cheerless, supercilious and stubborn last-ditchers. By the time they had sluggishly stirred and tidied us away into billets with nets, at least two erks had malaria. And one of these graduated to blackwater fever and, of course, died (raving).

So, on the third day, I was fed into a vacant bed in a huge tin cave like a shrunk St. Pancras Station. It was cool and dim and had no windows. The beds were about a stride apart and faced another line of beds across a widish gangway. When the nets were let down by the black boys, the place looked like an establishment for forty concubines.

As I've said before, opposite me was the MBC hand, the jetty-wallah, Pinkney and his oppo, Pouncey, a horrible fellow who wore mini-shorts that showed the cheeks of his bum like twin apples, a homosexual if ever I saw one.

Pinkney was cream with black hair and Pouncey puce with golden hair (combed forward). Both wore sunglasses practically all the time. Some called them Mr. and Mrs. Pinkney and some, Mrs. and Miss Pouncey. They were what psychology books call extroverts and had long, meaningless talks after Lights Out, but what they said was for us, not the other. Though erks used to yell at them to shut up, they really savoured it because it was a different kind from any talk they'd ever heard. And about a different world. I spoke to Pinkney once, but to Pouncey—never. Though I saw him die.

For a few days there was nothing to do, no kites to service, no-one to tell us what we were doing there, no-one knowing anything about anything. It was Blackfen all over again. But nowhere to escape to.

There was some reading done but only of the big rolls of *Daily Mirrors* and the pornographic books from market stalls you see pawed over by awful women ordered out by their husbands to buy substitutes more titillating than themselves. Some played cards for money, some wrote massive letters. But most slept and grumbled.

I was sitting on my bed on our fourth day about tea time when I heard an aircraft fly over, and the word went round that our squadron kits had come. We left our wankahs and rushed out and down the gravel road to the apron behind the jetty just as the first Catalina loped overhead, turned and began to its run down the Trot, gradually dropping its nose till it touched, slicing the water into plumes of spray and slouched on to a stop. And five minutes later, another followed, and then another and another until six were down and the MBC had towed them to their buoys.

Then the crew started to come ashore, festooned with their baggage and equipment, staring curiously about them, looking very pink and very professional. We stood and eyed them without saying much: flying was another world from us but these men were the cutting edge of our effort and, by and large, we respected them and wanted to give them satisfaction.

Next day a parade was called. They lined us up on the cricket ground while the officers, as was the peace-time custom, walked rapidly up and down in pairs like performing animals. Then there was some mumbo-jumbo from the Drill Manual and the flag was hoisted to more yelling, shuffling and bags of phoney saluting and stamping which I suppose they'd thought up to fill in the day during peacetime.

We apparently had a name, No. 697 Squadron, and our C.O., a wing-commander, addressed us. He seemed a sensible man. No mad-dog barking about the only good Hun being a dead one, or the 'Let's hit Jerry for six, fellahs' claptrap which we'd suffered at Blackpool from professional rabble-rousers recruited from mental homes for decayed officers. We were here to replace the Sunderland Squadron and to do two simple jobs, he said. (A) To help the Navy intercept blockade-runners, (B) to sink U-boats loitering in the approach to harbours or en route to India by the long way round the Cape.

'And it's jollywell not only the air-crew who will do this,' he said. 'They cannot jollywell fly unless your maintenance is first-class, absolutely first-class,' and went on, that after what happened to the *Mungo Park*, he needn't tell us that U-boats had to be jollywell put down. And he knew he could jollywell rely on us to do the work of the poor fellows who had been lost in that disaster. ('That little bit extra' he kept saying.)

Then we were told to go down to the Working Area and find our sections and get ourselves jollywell organised.

'It's like starting at a new school,' Wakely said. 'Well, we've soon seen the new Head. He seems jollywell civilised. But now for the prefects; they're always bl-l-loody. The

66

bastards rise to the top because they're better at lying, bum-sucking, bullying and sitting it out. I suppose the photographic establishment will be a corporal and three airmen—with an aircrew officer detailed to keep a general eye on things.'

He was right except for one thing. There weren't three airmen-photographers. Only us two; the other nameless one had stayed aboard the *Mungo Park*.

The Corporal was worse than we might have expected. He was a thin, pasty-faced chap with little eyes. He had a terrible moustache of very fine gingery hair and he wore an immense topee like a turned-up coal scuttle to protect him from sunstroke – he was almost bald. And his shorts were too long as though he'd just grown up. He was about Wakerly's age, a couple of years younger than me, and you could tell he'd not had his tapes long by the way he carried on.

'Are you A.C.2 Flanders?' he said to Wakerly.

'No, that's this chap, corp,' Wakerly replied cheerfully. 'I'm the other one—Wakerl-l.'

'Corporal!' he bawled.

'Corporal!' said Wakerly.

I didn't look at Wakerly. Whenever he was called to attention, he switched over to moron-control as he called it —like a clothes-horse, his shirt and shorts suddenly too long for him, a complete idiot look on his face like a simple-minded person who desperately *wanted* to understand and please. And his arms rigid and out slightly from his side, as though he was ready to shoot up like a rocket and, as I said, everything about him suddenly would be too big. I don't know how he did it, even his nose drooped and his fingers stretched to his knees to give him a positively ape-like look. Even the dimmest NCOs *felt* that he was taking the piss out of them but couldn't put a finger on exactly *how*. Years later, I recognized him in an illustration in Dickens's

Nicholas Nickleby, an abandoned youth named Smike, whom his persecutors always dressed in a small boy's cast-offs.

'Well, I am Corporal Glapthorn,' this little man said (dragging his eyes off Wakerly). 'And *my* photographic section is going to be the *best* photographic section on the coast of Africa.' He paused. 'Or I'll know the reason why. Is that understood?"

As we didn't reply, he shouted it again.

'Yes, Corporal,' we said. But I saw Wakerly's eyes flicker in my direction. He knew that before this Corporal Glapthorn stood the most incompetent photographer on this or any other coast of any continent.

'You,' he snapped at Wakerly, 'will be i/c during my absences at squadron tactical or administrative conferences. You are to log whatever transpires, note any personnel who visit and you are not to make any decisions. Is that understood?'

'Corporal!' cried Wakerly, stamping.

'Everything must be signed by me. And—you are not to utilise service time, equipment or materials for private photography. A breach of this will result in you being placed on an immediate charge. Each morning you will report for work at 8.30 hours and proceed to dust . . .' He went binding on for ten minutes, itemising the workhouse routine he'd spent the voyage working out in his little head. Then, he set us to clean the place from top to bottom whilst he sat at a table and pretended to look like the Chairman of I.C.I.

Suddenly he yelled, 'And Flanders, I *don't* like airmen without ambition. I DO NOT LIKE A.C.2s IN MY SEC-TION. You will prepare yourself for a trade test and I give you three months to pass as A.C.1. Is that understood?'

Apart from feeling it unlikely that, even given ten thousand years, I could pass the sort of trade test he was

68

likely to set, I tended to agree with him. A.C.2 in our trade was four bob a day. A.C.1 would bring in another half-dollar.

'Well,' I said to Wakerly as we trudged back to the billets, 'just our luck to get a stinker. Pass a trade test—that's a laugh. As soon as he finds me out, I'll be back collecting salvage or dusting the palm trees.'

'Just give him another couple of m-months,' Wakerly said, 'and he'll have put up so many backs that he'll be the camp leper. We're the only two who *have* to put up with him; the rest will kick him into shape for us. Besides, look at him! This climate'll crumple him. In two months he'll be what passes as normal and, in six months, he'll be mental. And besides, somewhere, there's an officer nominally in charge. If it gets really bad we can always p-petition him.'

Seven

You know how it is opening an innings on that kind of heavy afternoon when the new ball swings like a boomerang and the bowlers have their tails up. You need just enough luck to stagger through the first half dozen overs until you can weigh things up. At the Photographic Section, I didn't have that sort of luck and was ousted neck and crop in the first over. It was like this.

As a photographer it wasn't that I was stupider than most; it just was that, until I was called up, I was still at the No. 2 box Brownie stage and the telescopic training they gave me was just so much mumbo-jumbo. By the time they reached our entry, they'd worked through the rich seam of professionals and keen amateurs and were down to bedrock. To give credit, they tried their best and retooled the conveyor belt just aiming to produce labourers capable of blindly going through basic motions. Wakerly, with his schooling and university, could grasp what it all was in aid of but, most of the time, I just blindly bashed on hoping for the best. I can't say this too clearly—I'd every sympathy with Glapthorn at having me dropped on his doorstep. I know what it's like having even one incompetent in *eleven* in a cricket team: at the first panic he drops you in the cart. And here I was—one in *three*.

Really, most of the work was so straightforward you wouldn't think anyone capable of bungling it. It boiled down to being able to load a magazine, clip it on to an F24 camera and hand it over in its box to the navigator, wait till it came back, unclip this magazine, turn out the lights, lock the door, fit the magazine on to a developing machine, clip the lid and turn a handle. A machine with arms could have done it.

But frankly I never really understood it. My heart used to stand still, dreading making a mistake, certain that whatever I was doing was wrong. I suppose it's a kind of mental disease. I had an auntie the same. If she was last up, she'd go around all the outside doors and lock them and then go round again to see if she *had* locked them.

You could put me in front of fast bowlers dropping them short of a length on a wicket like a cart-track and I even felt a sort of joy defending myself and my bailliwick. But, alone with an F24 magazine in a dark-room, and my legs turned to jelly. There's one thing of course you have to bear in mind; you just make one mistake with a film, even a slight one, the fix instead of the developer, the wrong safelight switch, the merest flash of light—and the whole job is ruined. And can't be put right. There are no near misses in photography.

Until now, the Sinji kites had been coming back from nil patrols but on the particular night when, for the first time, I was on night duty alone, the crew of K/697 thought they'd spotted a neutral that could have been a blockade runner creeping northward (from the Far East) but couldn't positively identify it. I heard them talking it over as they came into the Ops Room with the camera about midnight. 'It was a Spaniard,' said the captain, a notorious man, F/O Gawkrodger-Jones, nicknamed Desperate Dan by the maintenance men because of the four or five bounces he usually did whilst landing K.

'Looked like the *Burgenland* to me,' the navigator said sourly '. . . dolled up like a Spaniard. As I told you at the time. . . ."

God, I could have run a mile. It was the second time I'd

seen that F24 that day; I'd cleaned and assembled it myself that morning.

'Well, how long will you be?' the Intelligence Officer asked. 'An hour?'

I said I'd be a little longer.

'Can't wait longer,' he said. 'You must tell me when it's washed and I'll have a quick look. If it looks promising, I'll get a signal off to Command and they can alert the Navy and the Sunderland detachment at Pointe Noire.'

I took the box as though I was humping my own coffin. There wasn't a soul about, nor, except for the buzzing of insects in the bush, a sound. As I opened the door to go in, the transport carrying the crew back to their beds slashed past. Then silence again as I locked myself in.

I switched on the green safelight (that was so dim that you couldn't see even it for the first few minutes) and detached the film case. Then I checked the tanks, saying aloud, 'Developer on the Left. Fix on the Right. Water in the Middle.' I took a last look round to establish for certain where everything was. Then I set the timing clock and switched off the roof light.

My hands were trembling and sweating as I released the magazine lid and began to feed the roll into the patent machine with handles on. 'Developer on the Left,' I said and sank it in, took a deep breath and began to grind until the alarm went off. 'Water in the Middle' . . . 'Five minutes washing.' I had to fight myself from taking the lid off to see if it was coming out OK. 'Fix on the Right.' Ten minutes of that. Then, against all the rules, I took off the lid and pulled up a length of film, turned it over as near the green light as I could push it and peered at it. Absolutely black. I pulled out a bit more. Black too. I could have wept.

Perhaps the stupid navigator ballsed it up, I thought. He must have. I rammed back the lid and began to grind again; this time in the water, but in a mood of utter hopelessness.

Then I took it out and pegged it to the end of the revolving drying slats, a slippery twenty foot length of film five inches wide; it's like wrestling with a sea monster. I switched on the power and this contraption went rattling round at breakneck speed. I gave it minimum time then switched on all the lights and really went over it. Black from one end to the other. Except for one exposure which was black but for one small corner, and that showed a tip of a mast.

Then I died a thousand deaths as I paced up and down. The job was done and by rights could stay on the slats till Glapthorn came on after breakfast. I knew that the Intelligence Officer would be hammering at the door in about ten minutes, so I let myself out, locked up and ran down the black road to the billet, found Wakerly's bed and shook him. He groaned and twisted but I got him awake and said he had to come because something had gone wrong. We hurried back together, neither speaking.

It had him puzzled. If it had been all black, I might have had it in the fix before I developed it, or I might have botched it up by switching on the main light whilst the film was out. It was that little corner showing the mast that foxed him. He said there was nothing we could do now at this time of night; he'd work it out in the morning, but it didn't seem to be anything to do with me.

As we were staring at it, someone began to knock at the shed door.

'Is that film ready yet?' It was the Intelligence Officer.

I looked at Wakerly. He looked a bit rocky himself for once, but he opened the door.

'Sorry Sir,' he said. 'I'm afraid there's n-nothing on this film. Perhaps the navigator forgot the motions in his excitement. I've known it happen before.' He pointed at the film looped round the slats. 'Sorry,' he said, 'it's a b-blank.'

The Intelligence Officer didn't argue the toss but went off to send his negative signal and then, I suppose, to bed.

That set me a bit more at ease and I went back to the billet and fell asleep. Then it was my turn to be shaken awake. By Glapthorn! He was as mad as hell. 'You're on a charge,' he hissed. 'Get off your wankah and up to the section, one-time.' When I arrived he was waiting for me like a figure of judgement. He'd brought up the camera from the Ops Room and had taken it apart. Wedged in the barrel, obscuring the lens, was a black duster. When I'd cleaned the camera before issuing it to the navigator, I'd put it there to protect the lens in case one of the bolts slipped and damaged the glass. The navigator might as well have pointed the F24 down a railway tunnel on a black night.

Looking back, I suppose Glapthorn could have pulled out the duster, and said nothing about it and reported he couldn't explain the failure. But no doubt he was afraid the C.O. might insist on the film going to H.Q. West Africa for the Command Photograph Officer to investigate, and he undoubtedly was such a clever devil that he'd have worked it out, and then Glapthorn would have got it ten times worse than me.

So he put me on a technical charge. I got the 'cap off, left-turn, halt' routine in front of the embarrassed pilot they'd detailed as officer i/c Photography and he gave me 7 days' C.B. and a talking to—'let you off lightly because of your inexperience,' . . . 'gravity in time of war' . . . 'we must all keep on our toes,' etc. The C.B. was nothing. Everybody at Sinji was permanently Confined to Barracks.

It was the shame of being marched there that got me down. That and Glapthorn rubbing it in. Whenever I had any sort of a job to do he put on his anxious-act. 'Promise me you won't make a hash of this, Flanders. . . . Not again, please,' he used to say. . . . 'Let's have your finger out, just this once.'

He got me into such a state, every time a film came in,

especially at night when I was on my own, that I went through hell, dithering and sweating, practically fainting with relief when I saw four or five consecutive exposures showing sea or shipping. I used to actually pray that, if ever a kite attacked a U-boat, I should have a fit or black-water, anything, to prevent me being the one who had to prove whether it was Truth or Fiction.

As it turned out, that was the only boob I made on The Coast. Basically, I'm very careful and, God help me, I learn from my mistakes (which is more than some do).

I've told all this because, even though I may not mention my work again, this was my bread-and-butter routine, my 'daily round and common task' (as the hymn goes). I don't want you to think they sent me to Sinji for a foreign holiday.

Eight

But, it has to be admitted, I wasn't making too good an impression. A man's reputation is all and those first few weeks were zero for me. Life goes like that. In waves. When you're on top, take what you can. Just then, it was the pit of the trough for me. I don't acclimatise to a situation as quickly as most. It's the same when I'm batting. The first couple of overs anything can happen. Then I get a grip on myself.

I don't expect to be believed but, in the longest spell of really hot weather I'd ever known, I caught a cold. The other erks laughed, but when I began to shiver they pushed me off to the M.O. He looked and sounded as callous as they'd trained him to be and put me on M & B. I was supposed to parade at Sick Quarters each day for a new supply of three tablets—one after each meal—but the orderly simplified his job by giving me a boxful ('to save you coming round, mate. They're a bloody miracle—kill the virus at its root and it just withers away. No charge to *you*. Bring me back what's left when you're fit').

But, despite this modern miracle, I didn't get any better. Worse in fact. Next morning I woke up with a fearful head as though somebody had bludgeoned me with a club. I crawled out for chop and then up to the Section, but I must have looked so rough that even Glapthorn sent me back to the billet, and there I lay flat out until it was time for evening chop, and then back to the bed again. I was like this for six days and getting worse all the time. In the end, my legs got too heavy to lift, and I stayed put twenty-four hours out of twenty-four.

Glapthorn kept calling and gloomily inspecting me. Sometimes, I could hear him speaking but always a long way off. Honestly, I couldn't even rouse myself to answer: everything felt twice as heavy—legs, head, the lot. Wakerly later said that he came and sat by me every evening and had managed to keep others from bothering by telling Pinkney and Pouncey that the M.O. knew all about me. It was like a dream. There were short periods when I came-to, and whenever I did, it always seemed to coincide with P & P's madhouse talk which caused an immediate relapse.

('But, dearie, when I think of my social life now . . . he wasn't a bad fellow but his girl-friend worked in a grocery shop . . . you needn't be jealous of that sailor I met on Bristol Suspension Bridge: I pushed him over . . .')

You might well wonder why I didn't go back to the M.O. For one reason I couldn't drag myself further than the lavatory, and the other was that any visit to Sick Quarters was an affront to your pride—if you had any left (I had). It was part of their training to nag at you like a scrounger to frighten you off from ever reporting sick again. What a shower that medical lot were! Anybody will tell you the same.

But, on the Friday, I forced myself up because, not being officially sick, they'd probably have sent the Station police after me if I hadn't shown up at pay-parade. I'll never be quite sure how I stumbled, topee in hand, for my money. But I did it, even dragged up a salute. In fact, all would have been right but for having to march back in a squad. It was only about six or seven hundred yards but, honestly, I couldn't make my legs move fast enough. So I shuffled along, head hanging, gradually slipping back through the column until I was in the last rank and, then, on my own. I never tried as hard even in a race to catch up with that

77

squad, but I just fell further behind, the gap growing wider like a ship going away from a drowning man. It was as if someone was holding my legs: I felt so weak and hopeless I could have cried.

Then round a bend came this Flight-Lieutenant type. I saw him like a man in a mist. When I was almost level I pushed up my hand to a pathetic salute but he pulled me up.

'Why are you not with the remainder of the detail, Airman?'

'I can't keep up, sir. I don't feel very well.' I was so whacked I couldn't raise my head.

'Stand up straight,' he barked. 'Get that head up. You're fluffing.'

'No, sir,' I muttered and managed to focus on his face.

Even in the fog I knew him immediately. Turton! The abominable man who'd pushed us aside at The Vine and taken Caroline and got himself commissioned. He must have known me as I knew him. But he didn't show it.

'Don't answer me back,' he snapped, 'or you'll be on a charge. Now, join your detail—at the double. Get moving.'

God, I could have killed him, yelling at me like that. Nobody had done it for years. I think I was so weak my eyes filled up. Probably as much from weariness as rage. Normally, I don't think the King himself could have got me running, but I was so ill I hadn't any resistance and went off at a shambling trot, like an animal in the circus ring, till I got round the first corner where I fell into the long grass and lay there, crying with weakness and shame, impotently telling myself that someday, someplace, I'd get even with this swine, Turton, if it was the last thing I ever did.

There I lay until I could raise enough steam to half crawl to my bed again. When Wakerly came that evening to see me, I knew I ought to tell him about this outrageous bad luck for both of us but, honestly, I couldn't even manage that. I was in a shocking state.

All this time, I'd been taking these M & Bs religiously three times a day waiting for the tide to turn, and I'd finished the boxful. But I couldn't even crawl to the M.O.'s for a new supply and, next day, lay there flat out, and supposed I'd had it. The odd thing was I knew that I was dying and didn't care. (I've never really been afraid of death since because, towards the end, you *don't* care.) And this was the day that I began to feel better and, next morning, I was nearly myself again. Then the penny dropped. I probably had ridded myself of the original infection after the first few tablets and, after that, they'd drugged me. Was I relieved! It taught me a lesson. For the rest of my life on the Coast I was determined never to be sick again and put myself under strict discipline—had a shower every day, spent regular spells in the earth closets and no lying on my bed in the daytime.

When I got back to the Section, one look at Wakerly was enough to tell me he knew about Turton. He looked downcast and lifeless.

'Why him?' he said bitterly. 'Of all the couple of thousand stations he could have been posted to—why here?'

I said that there'd been a thousand airmen at Budmouth so it wasn't really remarkable that, when the pack was shuffled, one or two were dealt to the same spot. I said I didn't suppose anyone else at Sinji had seen either him or us before.

'In that case,' Wakerly said, 'they won't mind saluting and sirring him. But I *have* m-met him before, and I do.'

'Well, it cuts both ways,' I said. 'He knows we remember one or two things: he'll not want it passed round what he got away with at The Vine. He'll steer clear of us. Anyway, he's changed caste. Being commissioned's like changing the colour of your skin.'

'Then you've got another th-think coming,' Wakerly said. 'At the miserable institution to which his father sent him to avoid mixing with his economic inferiors, at least they learnt one thing thoroughly—to bluster and bully anyone who can't fight back, then to keep on stamping until whatever's beneath stops wriggling.'

'Well, all right,' I said. 'We'll see.'

But I was sure that I was right. Officers moved at a different level. They didn't have to battle it out with orderly room sergeants and guard rooms. They *looked* superior and, out there, they had natty short-sleeved jackets with brass buttons whilst we had coarse, spongey shirts with drab rubber buttons, a stamp of slavery. Most of them wore creamy stockings and that's what I particularly coveted: I've always been keen about stockings. For instance, I can't wear silk ones or cotton ones: they have to be thick, woollen and light in colour. (Shoes too—I have to have them a size too big so that I can prise one off with the toe of the other without unlacing them.)

Out there, on the peninsula between the bush and the sea, there would be no getting away from Turton because a squadron revolves around its adjutant. He gets to know all that goes on and just feeds the C.O. what he asks for or what he decides to let him know. Everyone, officers included, knows he's the C.O.'s front and that you must keep in with him if you want to get anywhere. Everything passes under his nose—signals, orders, postings, complaints, the lot. And he can break or bitch you up, and you can't do a thing about it. So Wakerly's prophecy *had* to be wrong.

But I could see that he was badly shaken and later, I came to see that, from then on, he was doomed. Turton brought back all he'd lost when he lost Caroline Driffield and it ate into him like a canker till he was corrupt.

Well, I was wrong and he was right about what we were in for because, when I went back to work, Glapthorn made a point of letting me know that the new adjutant, a Flt./Lt. Turton, had visited and instructed him never to hesitate to put me on a charge if he thought I was malingering, and then he'd let Glapthorn know that he'd read the report on the duster-in-the-barrel charge.

Actually, the Corporal was worried too. He'd twigged that Turton had more than a clue about photographic sections and was going to take too personal an interest in this one. And we all were still pondering our misfortune when in he comes. Turton himself. We all three came to attention.

'Is A.C.2 Flanders back at work, Corporal?' he said.

'Yes, Sir. I was about—'

'Any future failure to parade must be reported immediately to the Orderly Room. Understood, Corporal?'

'Yes, Sir.'

'Carry on then.'

He didn't move. There was an awkward pause. Glapthorn looked confused.

Then he said, 'Flanders, sprinkle the floor and sweep up. Take care not to raise dust.'

'Yes, Corporal,' I said and got a brush.

'And L.A.C. Wakerly, clean and load cameras C. and F.'

'And don't leave a duster in the barrel,' Turton said. Then he went.

How horribly right Wakerly had been. He was going to outface us, get us down—and stamp.

Nine

Looking back, I know now that Wakerly started downhill from that time on. He began to brood and that's always bad unless it leads to bold and determined action. (Like the great Lillywhite who said, 'If I was to *think* every ball I don't suppose they'd ever make a run.') He began to go for what he called 'little strolls' and I went along for company. We didn't talk much and always went the same way—out of camp and down the long gravel road which led to a Wog village, Jassyville, and then we plunged off into the tracks. Africa is full of these tracks because the blacks are the world's last pedestrians. A push-bike there makes you an aristocrat.

He used to walk too fast for my fancy because I like staring around (as most North and East Riding folks tend to do). And Africa is full of things to stare at, women with faces eaten half away, mouths gaping from temple to cheek, men with elephantiasis, their testicles hanging to their knees, or sometimes a leg or an arm as thick as a tree trunk. And there were flowering trees, festooned like wedding-cakes, ant-hills big as haycocks and, at night, fireflies in bushes like bonfires.

Africa at night! A black place! Here and there a dim oil lamp in a house or only a candle flickering. And voices in the night, people moving, giggling, but not seen. The blacks are great ones for standing absolutely still, like sticks or shadows, without a stir or flick of an eyelid. Looking at you. Not like U.K., everybody fastened in their houses or in pubs or at the pictures, secret and private. In U.K., even when you are dying and don't care any more about anybody staring, they put a screen around you.

But here on The Coast, the blacks begat and gave birth, beat their wives, prayed to their gods, wept, ate and died as though life was a football match where you bought tickets for a touch-line view.

Those were the kind of 'strolls' Wakerly and I took. He was beyond me. I knew it then. Our minds worked at different levels. It was what university had done for him. When you come to think of it, it's amazing we got on as well as we did and for as long as we did. Until Turton turned up again, it was perfect. That's saying a lot, but it's true. Sometimes we'd walk for a couple of hours and not exchange a word. O.K., he'd loved Caroline. He still loved her. But could he complain? He'd never told her he did. Who knows? Maybe she felt the same about him. Maybe she didn't. Who can tell? Women are strange that way. Nothing venture, etc. . . . I've noticed it times. Things look mad, impossible. You're just about all in but stick it out and, all at once, the tide turns. Look at it this way—can you tell what's going on in the other man's mind? Perhaps he's thinking of throwing his hand in too.

It boils down to who has the stronger will. Like facing a really good bowler. He knows that he has to wait till you make a mistake. Sometimes it's murder. Ball after ball on your leg stump or going away towards the slips. Your instinct is to let fly and, if you do, it gives him heart just when he's losing it. But stick it out and he thinks, I'll never get this bloke out, and it shows in his bowling. He gets wilder and begins to throw one or two loose ones down. I could kick myself the number of times I've opened an innings and sensed (as anybody can who keeps his wits about him) that their captain was going to take off his opening bowlers. Then the clot at the other end throws his wicket away and up go their tails, and the hard graft has to be done all over again.

I mean, why need Wakerly have given in at The Vine? He was the better man. He had more brains than Turton and he'd had a better education. He spoke well, his folks were the right sort, he had a good job waiting in civvy street. It boils down to this: he didn't stick it out.

We talked about it the once. One night on the tracks. Neither of us had spoken since we'd left the camp.

'We made a mistake at Budmouth,' he said. 'We shouldn't have let Turton push us off without a fight.'

'What?' I said. 'Do you mean at The Vine?'

'Caroline,' he said.

'We?'

'You were keen on her too.'

'She was out of my league.'

'She liked you.'

'Maybe. But only because I knew my place.'

'She wasn't a snob, Tom. You know that.'

'I didn't say she was. But I knew what the form was. If I'd begun to breathe too hard . . .'

'Don't be such a bloody fool,' he said.

'Listen,' I said. 'Don't work it off on me, chum. *You* know and *I* know that it was between him and you. I wasn't in the running. You knew it, she knew it, I knew it. You *let* him beat you.'

He didn't speak for about a mile more. Then he said, 'Perhaps you're right. No-one's fond of the truth unless it's pleasant. And the depressing thing is that, if it was all to happen again, I'd probably do just the same. It's a defect of character.'

I didn't reply but tended to agree with him. It's not a weakness I suffered from, but I wasn't too proud about that rough side of me. But there was this to be said for it—it

84

came in useful against bastards like Turton, those who could only understand a smart kick in the crutch.

One thing may strike you as odd: we never talked about sex, the wriggle and wrestle part of it. Caroline meant more than just that to him and it meant nothing to me.

At that time, I didn't think there was anything odd about it. Only much later. Now, I wonder if I was normal. *Then*, I used to congratulate myself. *Now*, I'm not so sure and wonder if it wasn't to blame for the obsession I later got about my cricket team and Turton. Talking to chaps now, it sticks out a mile that a number of them would have given their ears to have had a chance to set up an off-the-camp establishment with a couple of black concubines.

The lights of camp came in sight, then the guard room, then the cook-house. Lanterns were hanging from the cross posts of tents, erks were boozing, dozing, scribbling sob-stuff back to Wigan, Wellingborough and Weston-Super-Mare. A mob was emerging from the big hut which served as church, recreation-room and concert hall. This night it was Tranter's Troupe, a home-made sex-and-sob show put on once a fortnight. We were out of Africa again.

Just outside the billet he laughed. ' "The bitter, old and wrinkled truth," Tom—remember?'

Work that out.

Ten

It was all this sort of thing, following as it did Turton's bullying and the shame of being on a charge, that turned my mind to cricket . . . something that I could cope with. The parade ground was right in the middle of Sinji and it was the cricket ground too. There wasn't a blade of grass on it and, once past a fielder, every shot was a certain boundary—the ball ran like a hare on the baked earth.

I used to sit under the acacia trees watching the games. There was a league of sorts run by the Station Sports Committee whose Chairman was a young officer called Ruskin. The Ground Defence, Motor Boat Crews, Cookhouse, Gash Trades etcetera, used to play one another with energetic incompetence. (My wrists ached to get at some of the slop they called bowling.) Then there were the big boys—The Liberator Squadron at Zif, The Supply Base, the Sinji 1st Team, a couple of Army units camped ten miles away and the Navy; all these used to play 'friendlies' (though that was a laugh because Africa either put you flat on your back or else brought out the very devil in you).

As I picked up in myself, I felt a strong desire to play again. I hadn't played a game since Mr. Ridd's team back at Budmouth. As a photographer, I should have joined up with the Gash Trades, but you know how difficult it is to get started on things, and I always felt ashamed touting for a game: so I left it.

But, one day, I was sitting under this acacia tree watching a couple of teams scratching about like old hens on a midden and I was next to a 697 rigger called Slingsby. We got talking and I twigged his accent as West Riding—Ossett it turned out to be . . . and he said that he hadn't played the game since grammar school, because he'd gone in with an uncle who had a big draper's shop and Saturday afternoon was when they made the big money (more than the rest of the week lumped together). But he said that he venerated cricket (his words) and knew one or two others on the Squadron who would like a game and couldn't get one because all the teams were fixed up and really didn't want much to do with the new boys of 697. He spoke very ponderously as though he were selling a fur coat to an alderman's wife.

'You know,' I said, 'I've seen you before somewhere.'

Most people would have grinned, but all the time I knew Slingsby I only heard him laugh once (during our last innings together).

'You mean you don't know,' he said.

'No. Should I?'

'I'm the one you stopped sliding back into the hold when the *Mungo Park* went for a burton,' he said. 'It was you blocked me on the stairway. Aye, just when I was about over the boundary.'

Of course, I knew then. He'd been upside down. But I ought to have remembered his eyes—that respectable, crazy glare they had.

'Do the same for me on the way back to U.K.' I said.

Then it came to me like a flash that this was just the right chap I needed. 'Look here,' I said, 'we'll get an eleven up from the Squadron and find ourselves a few games. Unless you mind much, I'll be skipper and what about you taking on secretary?'

It may sound a bit brutal the way I put it—no mention of a committee and elections. But cricket was something I understood and, even as I sat there, I knew exactly what I meant to do. And this was to put together a team which

87

would beat every other side in the Colony. (I felt quite light-headed at the idea.)

He took the bait. It turned out that he had a powerfully developed liking for authority, and I bet he kept his sales-girls on their toes. 'But the snag is,' he said, 'I'm only a Leading-aircraftsman and you're an A.C.2 and the officers wouldn't stand for that: they'd want to run things; they always do.'

I was ready for that.

'Ah, but our team won't set itself up to be *The* 697 Squadron Team; we'll keep it a little private club and call it A 697 Squadron Eleven. The vital thing is the A—nobody can object to a little clutch of chaps fixing up a bit of a game for themselves.'

I could see him pondering this and then having a quick, second look at me, weighing me up. It's a way West Riding folk have. Then we went off to my billet to draw things up.

This Slingsby would be about twenty-one but looked and acted like a middle-aged widower. I expect he couldn't afford to behave young when he had a flock of girls to chivvy six days a week, the cheeky sort you get in the West Riding. He was tall and had a long set face, black hair neatly parted and exceptionally blue eyes. Looking back, it was these eyes you remembered. They had a sort of mad look as if there were two Slingsbys, one inside the other trying to get out. He was the sort you read about (happily married, five lovely children, J.P., next in line for mayor) who sud-denly drops everything, goes off to California and starts a new religion with himself as god. But, except for the eyes, straight-forward, honest, excessively neat, a real bank-clerk.

When you gained his confidence, he turned out to be very garrulous, in fact more than a bit of a binder, as he had only the two interests, his uncle's and his shop and his 'young lady'. The whole of his non-cricket conversation

88

rested on these twin pillars. There was one story about a sordid scoop in the supply of a rare variety of American ladies' underwear which he had pulled off (ignoring his uncle's advice) against the best brains in the London retail trade. Although I heard this story many times I've forgotten its details (except that they seemed to be an outrageous example of legal fraud), but I remember its climax came on the platform at Ossett Station, Down Level, when his uncle wrung his hand and declared (with 'tears in his eyes') 'Ah lad, ah'll admit it—tha were right and ah were wrong. Tha's bested them danged southerners; tha's a credit t'Yorkshire. Fra this minute thou'rt a junior partner in t'business.'

In his more mellow moods (after a good win) he talked about his 'young lady' (which is all he ever called her). She was a library assistant and went to the same chapel and she was petite and had certificates for things. (This was as far as he was prepared to share his vision.) He always spoke with reverence of her and he keenly regretted that she refused to become engaged to him before he was posted overseas. 'After all,' she had told him, 'one of us might change our minds; they say the Eastern women are very seductive.' I expect she meant this archly, to drive him into protestations of love. But Slingsby took it seriously. 'I mean,' he used to protest, 'can you see me wed to one of these black women. Can you?' Frankly, if ever the odd look in his eyes had got the better of the draper in him, I could—a big cocoa beauty caged in his little cash-booth to catch the flashing cylinders as they shot along their wires like massive pulls to square leg.

He didn't read books and, when he wasn't writing long letters to his 'young lady'—though I marvel, in Sinji, what he found to write about—he was leaning against his billet wall, cross-legged and crocheting a duchesse-set. God knows where he'd learnt it. Crocheting! Perhaps it's a folk-art in those parts . . . or perhaps it was part of a night school course on drapery.

Well, that was Slingsby.

And, having settled the main part—me captain, him secretary—we set about assembling a team. We had a trial match of sorts and it boiled down to one good batsman (myself), two very good bowlers (Slingsby and an instrument-basher known as Trader Horn), one brave and agile wicket-keeper and two Londoners, Wood and Stone, who looked as though they learnt to play with home-made bats and a cork ball in a council school playground; they had no strokes at all but were determined. The rest were an assortment who hadn't much clue but were willing and could run. Wakerly said he'd umpire if I'd go through the rules with him.

I had it worked out that it was necessary to win a couple of games to build up esprit-de-corps and confidence. So I carefully arranged our first fixture with the Stores Section who were a ropy lot of idlers. Their captain was a Welshman and he could only bowl. We beat them easily—by ten wickets, because we got them out for thirty or so and Wood and I knocked them off; at least I did, while he just stayed in. You have to remember that Slingsby and Trader were really very accurate bowlers, the one bowling what amounted to fast off-breaks, and the other was a left-hander who chipped them away towards the slip field, which anyone knows is the deadliest kind of ball. (If it doesn't take your off bail, you can snick it into any one of three pairs of waiting hands.)

After that game, we had a meeting and co-opted Wood, Stone and Wakerly on to the committee. It was no use asking Trader. He wasn't really interested in cricket; he was just a naturally good bowler and I bet when he left The Coast he never played again. What a waste!

Meanwhile, a Turton purge had begun and others at Sinji besides us were feeling him grinding on their necks. The C.O. was a flying man and not interested in admin and let his adj get on with it. On top of that, he'd been on The Coast a twelve-month and was losing his grip. So, when Turton tired of bullying the Photographic Section and his own Orderly Room, he looked for other victims to organise.

Well, there was always plenty of fat in the RAF to carve at, and one of the first things he *organised* was billeting. When men arrived at Sinji, they more or less fell on the first empty beds they found, so that trade sections were scattered round the huts and, for example, any N.C.O. looking in an emergency for his fitters, would have to do the rounds of half a dozen places, no joke in the middle of the night. Turton ordered a massive All Change—all sections to sleep within spitting distance of each other. It made sense, and it was a Plan (which always is a good thing). But the unco-operative erks wouldn't be planned.

'It doesn't matter where you go,' Slingsby told us, 'they're playing hell. In our billet they've got to fighting. It's bad enough having to put up with some binder when you're out on the kites, but to come back and find him still round your neck on the next bed! That stinker, Jones, stuffs that genius kid of his at university down my throat day *and* night, now.'

And I expect Jones was saying the same about Slingsby and his 'young lady'.

The biggest fuss in our billet was from the card fiends. They'd all been dealt into different billets and now were forced to make elaborate arrangements to meet and then it turned out a couple of Baptists had been moved into their midst and objected to (a) the noise and profanity and (b) the gambling. So it ended in fighting.

So Turton soon slipped into Lady's Astor's place as a

target for popular frenzy. He must have heard about it in the Officers' Mess, but it evidently didn't shake him because he proceeded to institute something even crazier. In its way, it tells you volumes about him. He ordered that a bugle should blow Lights Out at 10 p.m. each night. Like Beau Geste. I'm ashamed to say I rather liked it. There was something melancholy about it and a link with our Empire's former generations overseas. Not that I had much chance to hear it as I'd always imagined—a hush falling across hills and over water as the plaintive call died away. ... Because, at the first notes, there were mad shouts and screams from the surrounding night ...

PUT A PLUG IN IT ... TAKE THE BANANA OUT ...

YOU BLOODY SYCOPHANT (from the better educated) ...

I COULD FART BETTER THAN THAT ...

and immense razzes and hysterical howling. And the lights didn't go out anyway. In fact, everybody made it his business to switch lights not on already.

After about a week, the bugle was stolen and, though the guardroom wallahs poked around half-heartedly, it didn't turn up again, and I expect archaeologists will find another problem in some West African swamp in 2 million A.D. It will make a nice chapter heading in a thesis—The Lost Sinji Warrior Race. ...

Eleven

Things weren't going too well with our cricket club, although the playing part was going to plan. Besides the Stores Section, we'd beaten the Motor Boat Crews despite their accurate fast bowler, Angus, who was in the Station XI, and also the Gash Trades and one or two Sections such as the Electricians. Personally, with only three real cricketers and eight makeweights, I found it a real thrill— the same thrill as a tightrope walker must get as he looks down into the darkness before he inches out his first foot. I believed that, though the book was a hundred to one against pulling it off, it *could* be done—so long as my nerve could stand it and I kept to a plan.

If you're thinking, What about The War against Nazi Tyranny all this time? well, there at Sinji, it seemed far away and somebody else's business. You have to remember that, for most servicemen, War was only brief spells of intense effort or fear lost in a yawning wilderness of boredom. And we coped with this boredom in our different ways. With the little soldier at Blackfen and with thousands more like him, it was women, with others—beer, with me— cricket.

I didn't mention my idea of going on winning until we'd beaten everybody—this included The Liberator Squadron *and* then the whole lot rolled together, the Sinji 1st XI— even to Slingsby. It would have alarmed him. Instead, I concentrated on this plan which, for a start, was to build up the side's confidence. Then, if we brought it off, perhaps they'd tumble to what they'd been doing. And, anyway, why not?

93

Trader and Slingsby were good. Let there be no debating that. They were what bowlers ought to be and usually aren't—tall, strong, accurate, persistent, aggressive. They delivered the ball from a high arm action that lifted it above pad height. But no-one, not even themselves, ever realised that these two—as a pair—and used intelligently, were the most effective getter-outerers at Sinji.

But the batting! Except for myself, the rest were clueless. Put it like this—they were council school products. I suppose some teacher, at some stage, must have told them to push their left legs forward and to get over the ball and had talked vaguely to them about off-drives and square cuts, and they'd tried to carry out his words of wisdom on some cart-track smoothed over by a silly lawn roller. And the next thing they knew, they'd got a fast ball smack in their faces and, after they'd come to and for ever after, found it safer to keep their heads up and slash blindly. It's part of the social system. Down south, only the sons of the rich can play a forward defensive shot and keep their teeth.

However, the will to win compensates for a certain amount of technical deficiency and so, as I said, I concentrated on morale. We used to hold frequent committee meetings on my bed. Slingsby had done a course in business efficiency, (he planned to extend his drapery business to branches in Heckmondwyke and Cleckheaton when the War ended). So he used to keep minutes full of detail, 'So and so said this . . . So and so said that,' and then read them aloud with heavy satisfaction at the next meeting, methodically sounding all his aitches. All the others looked surprised to hear their names being read aloud, as no-one had ever bothered to record their views before. We had plenty of time and that filled it. Besides, it made everybody *think* cricket.

But, in another way, things weren't going too well at all; we weren't getting any sort of co-operation from the cricket

'Establishment,' that is, The Station Headquarters. Just the reverse in fact. Whenever we asked to use the ground for practice, they naturally put obstacles in our way, but where they really had us was over kit—they wouldn't lend us any bats except for pukka games. Not for practice. And you couldn't buy bats, balls, pads and such vital tools in the Colony in Wartime. They were sent out as part of the Issue, like food, to keep us fit for fighting.

And the S.H.Q. spiel was that, if they were used too often, they'd wear out—and where did the next lot come from? It sounds convincing, but you could tell there was more to it than that from the pleased way they said it.

It wasn't Maidstone, the Station captain, he was a true cricketer and no meanness in him. No, the chief plotter was this officer, Ruskin, a mean sort of man as I thought then, who had taken it on himself to run the Station XI. Once or twice I thought he'd worked out what I was aiming at. But I decided that mine was so fantastic a scheme that no-one *could* guess, until after it had happened. So I came to the conclusion that it was just natural bloody-mindedness—697 Squadron were new boys and he meant to keep us down. You could tell it from the way he picked the Sinji XI. If Slingsby was picked, then Trader and I weren't. If Trader was picked, then Slingsby was dropped. If I was picked, Trader and Slingsby weren't. Never more than one of us played for The Station at the same time. And he had a real bastard to help him—S.H.Q. sergeant called Fife, one of those stubborn stinkers they breed faster than mice north of Berwick, obstinate, cunning, utterly selfish. He wasn't a bad bowler, fast and determined—very hostile; he bowled as if he hated you. This was O.K. It's the way all fast bowlers should bowl. But, after a game Fife still hated you. And he made it his life's mission to stop us getting any kit or time on the ground. Of course, you get a lot of that in Sport. The Game comes first! That's a laugh!

95

The lads used to get wild about it, especially Slingsby who had a strong strain of Methodist indignation, and the two Londoners, Wood and Stone, these being well sown with the seed of rebellion; it being in Londoners' bones as history books make clear.

But I counselled patience and offered to repair the kit. This was turned down. So we had to get the Squadron chippy to make bats at half-a-dollar a time from local timber (willow doesn't grow on The Coast). They stung shockingly; if you tried to drive, it was tantamount to getting a violent electric shock up the arm. And they split as well. All you could say for them was that they were better than nothing for practising with.

Looking back, I'm not proud of one thing: as cricket got hold of me again, Wakerly and I drifted apart. He didn't seem to start interests out there as he had at Budmouth; he even stopped reading. I would find him sitting on his bed, his back against the wall and his eyes shut. He was too well brought up not to answer but he was lifeless: you had to work too hard at conversation. Even reminding him of Blackfen didn't raise a smile any more. Once I tried to spark him off by reminding him of the beautiful blonde, the one in the red mac, the girl without shoes on a wet night. But all he said was, 'Poor kid! I wonder how she got into that state? Beneath all the bravado she must have been desperate, pushed to the wall, no way to turn. She was probably as sick as hell, and all most of us thought about was how we could take advantage of her.'

There wasn't much you could reply to that. It was Turton, eating like a canker into him.

'Oh, for God's Sake, Tom,' he said after a minute, 'I'm sick of myself. What's it all about?'

'What's what all about?' I asked.

'This! Life! What are we doing here?'

'On The Coast?'

'If you like.'

'Well, what do you mean, if you didn't mean The Coast?'

'Oh, let it pass,' he said.

We'd lost touch.

But perhaps I'm not being fair to myself. I *did* try. Maybe not as hard as I should. It was beyond me: it needed somebody of his own sort. I left it at that and picked up something and tried to read it.

Then, next day, the mail came and there was a letter from his mother to me. She said though she didn't know me, Peter had written about me and she knew I was a friend and that he 'thought highly' of me. She went on to say they'd not heard from him for eight or nine weeks despite three letters written to him, and would I write back and tell them if anything was wrong because she was the worrying kind. But that I wasn't to say she'd written.

I couldn't very well write that he'd begun to booze with the Canadians who were a miserable lot of moaners, never satisfied, always binding on about being volunteers-but-not-for-this. I couldn't very well write that he'd thrown his hand in, had let a swine called Turton beat him. I couldn't write that, whenever he could scrounge a lift, he went off on his own to the town, and that I could guess what he did there.

So I told her that, like the rest of us, he was finding the climate trying but really was quite fit and that he probably found it hard to imagine that anyone could be interested to hear about the boredom of Sinji life. 'As a matter of fact' I wrote 'I'm glad you wrote because I've not written home myself for six or seven weeks and now I'll do so more often . . .' This wasn't true, of course; I wrote to my mother at least once a fortnight, not a great deal, chiefly answering her own news of folks in the district.

Well, I thought, who'd have thought it would come to

this—me looking after Wakerly! But her letter worried me and, next day when it happened to be my turn to be picked for The Station in a game against the Navy on their ground in the town, I asked the skipper if there was a spare place on the lorry and asked Wakerly to come and he said he might as well. ...

But I'd boobed badly: I forgot that Turton had got himself picked to play too and would be in the party. Wakerly was almost back to normal, looking forward to the trip—until he saw Turton sitting in the same lorry. Then he went back into his shell and screwed round, so that it appeared he was watching Africa winding past as we bounded along trailing a swirling wake of sand and gravel. And when we reached the Navy's ground—a magnificent grass field cut like a bowling green—Wakerly hung about looking lost and, though I always made it a rule with me to *think* cricket just before a game (I even used to carry a little file-end around to sharpen my boot spikes but, actually, to keep my mind on the business in hand.) . . . this time I got into my kit and, feeling a bit fed up about it, went and sat on the grass with him until Maidstone had tossed and lost.

Well, the odds were against us. None of us had played on a grass wicket since U.K., and our bowlers were pitching the ball short as though they were still on asphalt and matting. The Navy batsmen just lay back and *pulled* them and, when Maidstone packed the leg boundary, they lay back and *cut* them through where third-man should have been. They scored 43 off Turton's three overs and declared at two hundred and odd for three.

At tea, I took a plateful and a glass of squash and shared it with Wakerly (who wasn't due for any) and we nattered about Glapthorn or something until I put my pads on to open. Fancy! Before an innings—thinking about Glapthorn! When I should have been concetrating on how to cope with a grass wicket! Anyway, on my way out to the

98

middle, I did get as far as praying they hadn't an accurate opening bowler so as to give me time to acclimatise myself to the change of speed and a lower ball.

But no such luck! I took first strike hoping for one or two loose ones as often happens: instead, he was spot on from the whistle, pitching away-swingers from my off-peg, while I prodded away like an old hen . . . and missed. Looking back, (I've played that innings a hundred times since) I know now that I should just have covered my wickets and lifted the bat away from anything outside them. Swingers can't keep it up for ever, first there's one wild ball an over, then two, then three. And all the time you're seeing the ball better and getting in rhythm with the pace. It's just pertinacity.

But that was the day I didn't have any. The seventh ball —we were playing wartime eight ball overs—I hung out my bat like the washing and First Slip was tossing the ball into the air and everybody was bawling, 'Good ball!' when they should have been sneering 'Horrible stroke!' It was plain surrender and I deserved to be shot. Next over, Maidstones leg stump did three backward somersaults and, after that, it was a procession. All out for 55.

I didn't feel fed up about it as I would if it had been my own team. The will to win was lacking and the captaincy never bit into the game enough to swing its course. Like most captains, Maidstone had been elected because of his personal skill plus a massive good nature which caused no offence. He nodded gravely, he spoke slowly, it was generally believed that he was *sound*.

The lorry had gone off on another job and so Ruskin told us we could meet by the Victoria Hotel in a couple of hours time.

Twelve

The town was only a big village by English standards and a broken down spot at that . . . I don't know what it was like before we took over a hundred years ago, but it beat me where the Blessings of Civilization were that our village headmaster used to bleat about. (The ones we were supposed to hand out like the lady of the manor.) They didn't even have proper W.Cs. nor drains. They just chucked their filth into the street and relied on a passing vulture to bear it off.

These horrible bald-headed monsters seemingly were on the Rates and couldn't even be shouted at, let alone shot. There was one to each street, like the old men who guard art galleries, sitting hunched up to watch what goes on. When the offal was tossed out of a house, they struggled up from a rusty roof into the air and lurched across, inspected it, devoured what suited them and then flopped back. They were so heavy the corrugated sheets shuddered.

'But for these airborne beasts' Wakerly said, with a flash of his old wit, 'it's like B-blackfen with the central heating on. What a pile we could make flogging vultures to boroughs with strong Ratepayers' Associations!'

In the market, there were fat women sitting in the dust selling dried fish and other desiccated eatables spread on palm leaves. We were so hungry after beans and biscuit that I'd even have tried a mouthful but for the warning we'd had about dysentery.

'Hey, you two fine soldier-men, here what you look for' an immensely stout, cheeky-looking woman called. 'Kanjinut. Chew 'em. Plenty Vim then. Jig-jig two, three time a day. All girl love you. Call you Tiger Man. Plenty cheap. One nut, one penny.'

The other women giggled.

'What's she on about?' I asked.

'They're aphrodisiacs' Wakerly said, 'The Africans chew them to fortify their sexual vigour.'

He tossed a shilling and she counted a dozen black beans into his hand.

'You come my place' she said. 'I got two nice girl. Young. Clean. Never had man. Ten bob. One girl Rosie, one girl Lily. Treat you very nice.'

Wakerly laughed, began to chew a couple of beans and offered me some, but I said I could live without it.

Our next stop was the town's only bookshop (O.K. Zekki, Purveyor of libraries to Men and the Sons of Men') and it was empty. Not of people—of books. I think it must have been the only bookshop in the history of the world that sold out.

'It was Great Disaster to Mungo Park ship out there done it' he said. 'I had Big Order of many fine books indeed, of Great Variety to satiate All Tastes. All in Davy Jones Locker. Great nuisance! In this town many lovers of learning. But you I can aid. Oh, I see you are Scholars. One book under the counter.' Hereupon, like a conjuror, he produced Chapman & Hall's Theorems of Euclid to School Certificate Standard.

Wakerly laughed like a drain, but I decided that, if I couldn't understand them, I could always sell it to someone who had aspirations—like a Welshman. So I put down seven shillings and bought it. As Wakerly was talking to the man, I had a quick look in it. It began,

'When one straight line meets another straight line, the adjacent angles together equal 180 degrees.'

That sounded pretty inscrutable . . . but, as I keep saying, one commodity above all on The Coast was plentiful—time.

'Why ever did you buy that tripe?' Wakerly asked, so I pretended it was to keep my mind off sex.

'Well, I know a better way of damping the fires . . . if you'll wait for me,' he said.

So we turned off the main street into a lane and then into a compound fenced with rusted corrugated iron sheets. It was full of litter, and there was a lorry with its engine and two wheels missing, and flocks of skinny hens and bloated children chasing in and out of the mess. We went up to an unpainted house and a giantess, black and shiny like coal and with startling big breasts, let us in.

She had three bare girls sitting on a red plush sofa and they tittered and pushed their fingers between their legs, until she clapped her hands.

'They new in from Bush, gentlemen' she said. 'They got no refinement. Plenty vim. I teach 'em all tricks. All clean, nice girl.' Then she added something in African, and they got to their feet and strutted awkwardly up and down, turning round all the time. Wakerly touched one of them on the shoulder and took her off behind a frowsy curtain. I heard him plodding up uncarpeted stairs and imagined him miserably relieving his tensions on a sagging mattress supported by a bed that needed oiling, with three brass balls on the posts. (One was sure to have been stolen by a sacked girl for an anti-fertility charm.) I told the woman I'd wait and she sent the two rejects staggering off with a sewing machine—everybody in Africa has a sewing-machine.

Then a black French sailor came in and she spoke to him in French; telling him to cool his heels I expect. (That madam was quite a scholar; I suppose managing an Establishment pays better than school teaching.) He obeyed and sat on the edge of my sofa, staring at the back of his hairy hands and sweating with desire. To avoid looking at him, I examined the room. The biggest item was a radiogram and, above it, was a large coloured picture of King George V with Queen Mary towering above him. She had brilliantly pink cheeks and a very red mouth and he was laden with yellow medals. Then there was a portrait of Jesus, like a young Cheltenham curate in fancy dress for the Xmas Fayre, and a text below him—'DEEP CALLETH UNTO DEEP AT THE NOISE OF THY WATERSPOUTS'—and I was still considering what it meant when Wakerly reappeared.

As we went, I saw Madam motion the sailor to take over where Wakerly left off. Sharing even a black girl with a black revolted me. I still couldn't conquer my colour prejudice. I thought this was yet another defeat for Wakerly. It was awful letting himself be beaten like this. And really awful to think that all this had started from Caroline, that marvellous girl.

'Disgusted?' Wakerly asked.

'In a way,' I said.

'Go on,' he said.

'Well,' I said, 'would you like your sister to marry a black man?'

'Great God in Heaven!' he almost shouted. 'Not that from you, Tom! Really, you stagger me at times. But all right, if you want me to take you seriously: no doubt it would shake me. After all, let's face it, it has its bizarre side. But, if it did happen, of one thing I'm quite, quite sure. I'd rather my sister married an African than some ghastly white layabout or some halfwit snob or some hard, selfish stinker who worships his bank balance and his sports car or some vicious philanderer who would make my sister unhappy.'

I had to agree with him. So would I. Though I couldn't see myself getting off the train at Wintersghyll with a negress on my arm and going down the platform to meet my grandfather . . .

We made our way mournfully back through the hot slum. Wakerly's bounce on the brass-knobbed bed hadn't solved anything. A skinny little boy on a bicycle caught up with us, braked and rode slowly at our side, grinning and offering to guide us to his sister ('very nice girl see you O.K. only twelve years . . . know all tricks . . .'). I gave him sixpence and told him to buzz off. When he didn't I grabbed his bike so that he lurched crutchwise down the crossbar and then I tipped him off and let the bike fall on top of him. He began to yell something about police. . . .

The lorry was waiting outside the only hotel that looked remotely sanitary—naturally, it was Out of Bounds Other Ranks. We climbed up and sweated until Turton and Ruskin strolled out. Then we set off for Sinji.

Everyone was pretty quiet as we went along, depressed I expect, until there was a mechanical hold up under a mango tree. Then someone, (I think it was Sergeant Fife), stood up and picked a couple of the green fruit and shied them crashing at a wooden house end. Half a dozen others joined in and let fly at anything and anyone in sight. Some hit corrugated roofs like drum beats, one hit an old man, a child began to scream as he was struck on the back of the head as he ran for shelter. It was all hell let loose. These mangos were heavier than apples—more like cricket balls, except they burst when they landed. The blacks must have thought us fiends from hell. And Turton had joined in, shouting as loud as the rest. It was astonishing really, I suppose that he was letting off steam after the way the Navy had massacred his bowling and, at the same time, since he wasn't in charge of anything, he felt he could be one of the lads and pick up a spot of popularity. Of course, not everybody joined in. Maidstone didn't and a couple of others, and I was surprised to notice that F/O Ruskin sat looking straight before him (but doing nothing to stop it).

Mercifully the lorry set off again.

But the worst was to come. As you know, they don't have tap water in the villages, and the black women used to draw it from wells, balance the earthenware pitchers on their heads and then walk along the edge of the road, some of them as far as a mile, poor devils.

Now, lorries going to and from the town on this long, flat stretch of road, always carried a brush to sweep out the dust, and Turton picked ours up and began to do a billiard cue act with it, pretending to pot these pitchers off the women's heads.

Well, he got a few laughs, but the swine soon tired of cue-ing the air and began actually playing to poke off the women's pots. The first woman caught her jar before it dropped—but lost all her water. She looked terribly frightened. But the next one he hit, though she grabbed at it like a half-asleep fielder, first one hand and then the other, dropped it and the pitcher smashed, leaving her howling and half drenched in a puddle. Half the chaps were hooting, and about half were pretending not to notice. I guess some had enough imagination to see a crowd of blacks going through their home town and knocking shopping baskets out of their sisters' and mothers' hands.

I could see Wakerly's face twitching and when he got off his bottom and onto his knees I knew at once what crazy thing he was going to do.

'Ride it,' I muttered. 'We're nearly to Sinji.' But he angrily shook me off and crawled over to Turton, got close to his face and hissed something in his ear, then crawled back. In came the brush. No-one could hear because of the lorry's rattle, but everyone knew that something had happened. The laughing stopped and we finished the ride uneasily.

Walking back to the billet I asked him what he'd said.

' "If you do that just once more, I'll report you to the Commanding Officer".'

'Did he say anything?'

'No.'

'And would you?' I asked.

'Yes,' Wakerly said. 'He'd have got into a row and I'd have got into a worse. They don't let an airman get away with reporting an officer.'

'He's not going to forget it,' I said. 'Not Turton.' I didn't say any more; it was done now. In a way I felt I ought to have supported him but it was such a damned stupid thing to do. Who would gain from it? There would only have been time for him to have knocked one more pitcher, that's all. And these black women were used to rough treatment from their menfolk. It was their way of life to be knocked around, and, even if the more intelligent blacks got to know about it, this wouldn't make them want to be rid of White Men more than they did already. Besides, we photographers had to live with Turton and he had us just where he wanted. In U.K., we could have asked for a posting but, at Sinji, you couldn't escape for even a forty-eight.

As we reached the billet Wakerly said, 'The trouble with you is you're too bloody neutral. One day you'll climb off your fence and then we'll know what goes on in your swede-basher brain : I wonder which side you'll come down on. Sometimes, I think Turton and you are brothers under the skin—Fascists. And for Pete's sake stop calling these people 'blacks'—they have a country too. Call them Africans.'

He was upset. He didn't mean what he said, so I didn't answer except, 'O.K. . . . . O.K. It's a matter of opinion.' But I thought, Ah well, think what you like, but I'll wait for the right time before I settle with Turton and, when it does come, I'll choose it and the place and only when I'm sure of winning.

All the same, I was a bit upset that he'd compared me with Turton. He couldn't have been serious.

Thirteen

After that it was murder at the Section. Turton came snooping around every day, always addressing Glapthorn as though Wakerly and I were invisible . . . 'Is everything all right, Corporal?' 'Anything I ought to be told about, Corporal?' 'I insist on being kept in the picture, Corporal.' The trouble was that he was a good photographer, a very good photographer: he knew just where to look for mistakes.

Of course, he never mentioned the billiard brush incident —too crafty for that. He just drilled away at Glapthorn, criticising the quality of batches of prints, dust-specks on enlargements; once he even went methodically through the rubbish-can to find evidence of bromide-paper wastage on trial exposures. He'd weighed up Glapthorn and knew that he'd lose his nerve and would pass on the squeeze to us. The cunning brute knew that Wakerly could only take so much of this before flying off the handle, that he'd lash back at the Corporal who would then put him on a charge for insubordination and serve him up on a plate for Turton who couldn't then be accused of victimization. It was a diabolical.

And it worked just like that.

Oddly enough, I see now that Glapthorn half guessed something unusual was brewing, but I also see that he didn't dare to find out just what. He was wind and nothing but wind, not a thing to fall back on when the heat was on; a poor spiritless wind-bag: he withdrew from any practical work so that any mistakes had to be ours. It was lousy and weak-kneed, but then Glapthorn was Glapthorn.

Me, I felt that I could take whatever Turton dished out.

We had only to stick it out for another six or eight months and our time would be up on the Coast and, God willing, we'd never see him again. Besides, I was buoyed up by the hope that the chance might yet come when I could face up to him on my own terms. Admittedly, it wasn't much of a chance but you never know.

But Wakerly—he'd played his hand and he'd lost. All he'd succeeded in doing was to set Turton really going, bent on humiliating us. Why couldn't he have let things ride, kept his nerve, hung on until we felt something give? Really, it was just like a game: you could never tell when the other man would throw in his hand.

But Wakerly wasn't even in the fight any more. Between them, Turton, the booze and African women had got him down and, like Glapthorn, he'd nothing to fall back on. He'd been brought up too free and easy, his folks had explained away those things I'd been taught to abhor—sodomy, self-indulgence, sensual license, sin: *his* underpinning had gone. Now, I'm not too certain myself about things like that, and I don't know how I'd bring up a son if I had one. Sinji and what happened there cut the ground from beneath me. It was all right for my grandad, living as he did, nothing changing much year after year on The Vale. It was all right for me—*then*: I still believed. It was like the hymn, The Shadow of a Mighty Rock within a Thirsty Land—it was there, something you knew was Right and True. But there's a time to speak out and a time to be still. Like the rest, I can keep my head well down.

And when it came, it came suddenly. We were all there in the dark-room. I was doing some contact prints, Wakerly was processing enlargements in a big shallow bath with Glapthorn whittling away at his elbow—'You've over-exposed them . . . you're going to waste all this paper . . . quick, get that one out . . . use the tongs . . . you've finger-

108

marked this one . . . it's me that has to explain to Mr. Turton . . .'

That was the flash-point—'Mr. Turton'. The orange safe-light normally gave you a malarial look, but Wakerly's face was the colour of advanced blackwater. He drew in a long rasping breath, shoved his trembling hands into the dish, scooped up a sodden custard pie of photographs streaming with chemical solution and pushed the lot into the Corporal's face.

'You l-little s-snivelling, twittering t-toadie!' he yelled. 'T-take th-these to Turton: you can w-wipe his bottom with them. You're t-two of a kind.'

We all stood. Me still pressing hard on the printing lever, Wakerly startled out of his stupidity, Glapthorn shocked into utter immobility, the enlargements of sea and swamp, one by one, peeling off his face and slithering down his tunic to the floor.

Then we stirred, like coming from a dream. The Corporal bashed off to the Squadron Office to fill in a charge sheet, Wakerly miserably picked up the ruined work, I looked with astonishment at a print baked black.

Later in the afternoon word came from the Orderly Room that Turton would hear the case at the end of the week—Assault on a Superior Officer whilst on Active Service. On to the chopping block!

And later still, in the darkness, Wakerly and I tried to walk it off along the paths on the plain down by the river. We walked in silence. There was nothing to say. Turton had taken Caroline from him: now, he would strip him of dignity too. There *was* nothing to say. I knew it and spoke.

'You were daft to play the game to his rules. Why couldn't you have hung on? Things always change when you least expect. Your chance would have come.'

'You talk like a Christmas card, Tom,'' he said.

'Maybe I do,' I said, 'but I know it's the right thing to do.

Why don't you pull yourself together—drop the booze and stop going into town after native women?'

'O for God's sake, let's not have a sermon,' he shouted. 'Who are you to talk, you spineless prig! You seem to think that it's enough to keep your head down and the wind will stop blowing. You're as bad as Glapthorn. But bum-sucking is going to get neither of you anywhere. I know Turton's kind: the more you take, the more you'll get.'

I had an even temper or, at any rate, learnt early, living with Grandad, to keep it bridled. But it used to break out. Not often, maybe once a year. Afterwards, I used to be sorry because losing grip on yourself gets you no forrader. Now, I've no need to check it: that year at Sinji burnt it out like a clutch and for the same reason.

Later, I consoled myself for what I said by believing that I liked Wakerly so much and couldn't bear to see him plunging downhill—and for what? A lah-di-dah trollop, as randy as a farmyard cat in heat. Her and a self-centred bully.

'Listen,' I said, 'you want to grow up and come out of your dream world. And you want to topple Caroline Driffield off the pedestal you've put her on. Boarding at convent schools don't make them all into angels, you know. If she's a sample of what they turn out . . .'

Wakerly stopped and turned. 'What are you getting at?' he said.

Then I really went up.

'She'll lie in a hedge bottom with anybody so long as he can sound aitches. I saw what went on with Turton. It wasn't *all* him you know. He didn't need to take her clothes off. She'd strip the lot off without taking her eyes off him and grin like a cheshire cat while she did it. And then she'd start on him in the same order . . .'

I didn't see it coming in the dark when he struck me across the face with the flat of his hand.

'You filthy liar!' he yelled. Then he turned away and set off up the road. I think he was crying.

'Go on,' I called after him, 'run as fast as you like but you can't get away from it. That's what I saw and it's time you knew. I should have told you months ago. And, if you want to know, she'd have done the same for me. She tried it on. She'd have let you have it too if you could have looked at her without seeing a halo. . . .'

Then I pulled myself up sharp.

Well, this is it, I thought with dismay, the end of a friendship. Turton's split us and now he'll rip us one after the other.

We finished the road back to Sinji in silence; until we came to the Guard Room, it was too black to see and then I caught sight of his face in the light of the lantern hanging on their verandah; it was strained and pale. I knew I ought to say something to patch things up but I couldn't.

It was Wakerly who stopped and caught my arm. 'Tom,' he said, 'I'm sorry. I don't know what's the matter with me. I didn't know what I was saying. Forget it. You know how it is.'

He waited for me to say something, but I didn't.

Then he said, 'Was it true, Tom?'

'Yes,' I answered. 'But I wish now I hadn't told you. But, all the same, it's true.'

'God!' he groaned. 'I loved her and I can't forget, damn it.'

We stood for a while longer. Someone was shouting from amongst the tents. There was the usual buzzing in the bush.

'I can't,' he repeated, 'and I don't think I ever shall.'

Fourteen

I didn't meet Wakerly next day at the Section because he'd gone off early with K.697, Captain F/O Gawkrodger-Jones, alias Desperate Dan, to do a small mosaic of a creek a couple of hundred miles south which it was thought might do for squadron detachments to operate from. I was glad at being able to avoid seeing him until evening, and asking about the trip would break up the embarrassment of meeting again.

E.T.A. was 20.00 hours so I went off at about a quarter-to and hung around the Ops Room door. I was fed up to find Pinkney scrounging there: his place was on the jetty but he'd evidently decided that, since the crew boat and the fire-bowser had left for the Trot to await K, it was safe to slip up to Ops where it was light and cheery. Somebody had brewed up tea and a discussion began on the khaki crust which grew on the inside of pint mugs.

'It's a fungus,' said the Controller'—a minute bacteria conditioned over the centuries to resist scalding tempera-tures and tea. . . .'

'Ingrained dirt,' the sergeant said, looking meaningly at a clerk.

Know-all Pinkney had to push his oar in. 'Trouble is no hot water. Cold water's no use. Must have hot water. And soap. Absolutely basic for cleansing stained porcelain.'

'You've an answer for everything, Pinkney,' the sergeant said, 'and your place is down on that jetty.'

'When I was a boy-scout we scoured them with sand,' the Controller said flatly, 'and nobody would begrudge you sand around here.'

'Would scratch the glaze, sir,' Pinkney said. 'Then the mug would be open to infection.'

Everybody sat in silence, deliberating this professional statement. It was the last word and the discussion died.

After a time, the talk turned to living out with negresses but this too lapsed because the Controller looked sour (he'd only been here a few weeks) and began to talk about printing type-faces, gill-sans and baskerville.

Even Pinkney could scrape nothing to contribute to this (except to say profoundly that, before Caxton, everybody had good eyesight).

The Flarepath Officer, a Canadian, came storming in. 'Where were you, Pinkney?' he yelled. 'No-one down there to help us tie up. One of these days, so help me, you're on a fizzer. Goddam, it's blowing cold out there on the trot. Get the hell down there one-time, Pinkney, if you can't take a friendly hint.'

The radio operator began to whistle, 'I dream of Jeannie with the nut-brown hair,' and the sergeant began twiddling with the radio until he tuned to a short-wave programme from U.K., a hymn going in fits and starts, 'O happy band of pilgrims, If onward ye would tread.'

Then the wireless operator began to talk into the R/T.

'K for Kenneth. Are you receiving me? K for Kenneth. Are you receiving me?'

'I am receiving you. I am receiving you loud and clear.'

The flying boat was overhead now: I could hear the steady drone of her engines.

'I can hear you . . .'

'It's the flarepath dinghy signalling, you clot,' said the sergeant.

'No. Listen.'

They came to the door and we looked up.

There she was. Red and green lights turning. Nothing else. You had to imagine the great wing-span wheeling slowly at two thousand feet and the captain peering down at the ragged lines of lights bobbing on the Trot and the headlamps of an M.B.C. boat threading its way along them.

I thought, Fourteen hours out and he's brought her in bang on, dead on the target. Marvellous! A tiny, half-lit spot on the immense black coast of a continent!

I imagined Wakerly sitting amidships with his feet in the gangway, probably with the camera box between his legs, tying on his mae west and winding his absurd scarf round his scrawny neck.

I thought, We'll stop back-pedalling like we've been doing. If Wakerly had the nerve to turn on Turton, then I'm going to kick myself past him and ask to see the Squadron Commander and say we're being victimised. And blow the consequences.

I felt wonderfully pleased once I'd made this decision.

The beacon was lit. Under the water tower girders, the mobile power unit was popping away, one or two electricians were pottering around, the tower's shadow stretched away into the bush.

Perhaps I've given the impression that RAF Sinji was a cross between a Butlin's and Pentonville. Most of the time it was. But, for the record, sometimes there was a moment —like the deep roar of a kite overhead flying low as she came in to glide down to the creek—when you felt a sudden thrill to be there, with but an obscure part, in this great catalogue of war.

K.697 had turned south and must have been doing another circuit to lose height over the town so as to make its long slow descent to the creek. The engines were growing louder again and in a couple of seconds, out of our sight, suddenly the white spotlight would burst from its nose to illumine the water as she raced a couple of feet above the surface, till Desperate Dan dropped her bow to touch and then dig in, ploughing up furrows of spray.

But it wasn't like that at all.

'There's something queer,' the sergeant said. 'Glory! Listen to them engines: they sound wrong, they sound like a threshing-machine.'

We huddled at the door, between the light and the dark. The engines had merged into a confused roar suddenly ripped by a long-drawn screech. Then the silence almost hit you.

'She's pranged,' the sergeant cried. 'Poor sods!'

He was still shouting when there was a startling flash, and a sheet of fire shot up above the mangroves, blazed and then was dowsed like a match falling into water.

I galloped down to the jetty and reached there as a van screamed down the slope and the M.O. with two orderlies jumped out. A few seconds later the C.O. arrived. Pinkney flashed signals whilst the rest of us peered into the night. Then a boat came alongside and they tumbled in and raced off into the darkness. I hung around and soon fifty or sixty erks and NCOs were milling round.

All the boats were out and you could see their spotlights as they criss-crossed the Trot looking for survivors. When one came in to pick up a flight-commander someone shouted questions at the crew, but nobody bothered to answer. But it was passed round that three had got clear and five were missing.

In the darkness someone said softly, 'That bloody Desperate Dan: it was on the cards. It had to happen. I bet he was proving he could ride with his feet on the handlebars when it happened. They ought to court-martial him.'

Some way further off a cheerful tenor started singing 'Nellie Dean' but, alarmed by the furious shouts, changed to a low, defiant whistle. Somebody near me drew in his breath and pushed his way out towards the sound. It stopped.

I felt sick for Wakerly, wondering if he was alive or dead.

But we had to wait till midnight for even the first scraps of real gen. K had come in on a text book run but, when she was flying level twenty feet above the surface, she'd gone in like a stone, a fire started and her tanks blew up. Three had been hurled clear, injured but alive—(an African boatman had dived in and dragged out two) the rest had gone under with the Catalina.

We traipsed back to our billets and, when an M.B.C. corporal came in, he told us he'd taken the survivors at full throttle along the creek and river. He'd missed a floating tree by a hair's-breadth, his headlights had packed up, he'd navigated by the compass's light which half blinded him, he'd scraped into a dug-out canoe as it came up the wrong side. Then the army hospital wallahs had taken over. No, he didn't know if Wakerly was amongst them but one, the navigator, had tried to struggle free from his head bandages and another, a flight sergeant, was spitting blood and had died just through the hospital doors.

It was first light by now and I couldn't settle to anything, beside myself wondering if Wakerly had bought it. I went down to the jetty and they'd already begun to drag the creek. Two battered bodies were raised. But not Wakerly. Then the third and fourth floated to the surface. The news came in from the hospital that Wakerly wasn't there.

It was nearly sundown when he turned up. He'd been flung into the marginal swamp of an island amongst mangroves, but they said he was dead before he sank and that he wasn't burned. They gave me his scarf.

One of the chippies in our billet was working till after midnight on the coffins. 'It's a queer thing,' Pouncey said, 'kites crash and men get killed but next day the kites go off again and we're back again on a major inspection.' Someone tittered.

'Shut up, Pouncey,' said Pinkney, 'you sound like the fade-out of a U. film.'

'I know,' said Pouncey, 'I know,' he persisted. 'But it's true, isn't it?'

It was sickening to hear them.

But all the billets where tradesmen lived it was agreed that at least one good thing had come out of it—they would never again on a testing flight have to ride with Desperate Dan, and that this very definitely strengthened the odds on them seeing their native land again.

But they were wrong. A fortnight later the pilot of B/697 caught malaria and F/O Gawkrodger-Jones unpacked his suitcase and took over that kite and its panic-stricken crew.

Fifteen

They didn't bury you at Sinji; there was a military cemetery at the edge of the town in sight of the sea. This seemed a good thing to me as, near water, U.K. didn't feel too far off. It was very neat, like military graveyards always are. The sergeant had us brush down after the dusty journey on the back of a lorry, and then he marched us in. There was no-one there except an African sweeping a path and he removed what once had been a trilby and leaned respectfully on his brush; I suppose it was a rest for him.

The Chaplain had a deep voice and impressed us with his sincerity. He did it all very nicely—about the souls of the righteous being in the hand of God (who, I found myself thinking, I'd never heard—except that once—Wakerly mention). But unlike our chapel minister at home, he didn't say a few words over the grave. There being no relations present, I suppose it wasn't necessary. Anyway, I expect I was the only one present who knew enough about Wakerly to have said anything.

We fired our rifles into the air and, despite all the pep talk to 'do the job well, lads,' it was all at sixes and sevens like Guy Fawkes' Night. I thought how Wakerly would have appreciated this farewell RAF masterpiece. [Naturally, I didn't want to think about him but this Blackfen throwback struck me as the earth began to rattle down the hole.] To get him off my mind I wandered off and studied some of the other tombs and made a note of one or two on the back of an envelope from home:

118

IN MEMORY OF THOS. BOWLING, aetat 19, who perished untimely in the harbour from the effects of a season sickly beyond parallel in a climate pre-eminently fatal to the life of Europeans.

This small tribute is erected by the Officers of the Ship's Company, H.M.S. Fox.

They had experienced his Amiability and Work for two years and cannot but deplore his early Doom.

Well, I thought, I, too, have experienced the Amiability of Wakerly, as you might say, for a couple of years and now I have to go on without him, worse luck. But, actually, it was only as we passed the mango trees on the swaying lorry and met the African women humping their water-pots that I began to *think* about Wakerly and never having him around any more. I decided that we had *understood* one another, different as we were, and I recalled our conversations on Love as we'd idled among the salvage at Budmouth, his cries for help from Blackfen's flooded compound, how he'd put up with the Birdman and Blubber, his stammer, our Consumer Survey of Pubs, Hostelries and Inns and, of course, Caroline Driffield. And I thought his big trouble was being unable to force things to their right and proper end. He had charm, brains, background, but he lacked Turton's bite. And, as my grandad was fond of saying,

> 'If the serpent bite thee
> before it be charmed,
> What profiteth it
> the charmer?'

Damn him! Turton, I mean.

And, as I thought of this and looked at the faces of the

firing party drowsily jogging backwards and forwards as we lurched along, my eyes filled with tears.

As the days passed, his death became a dull ache for me. Ever since I'd met him stamping up and down Blackpool Prom he'd been part of this wartime life. To me, a Northerner, he'd opened up a new world, more refined than I'd known and he'd bothered himself about me. Probably not with much effect; but he'd tried to. And he was reliable. If he said he'd stick he'd stick and nothing would shift him. And he had confidence in me. He didn't really deeply understand cricket but he understood what it was made me persevere with that awful 697 XI, that to win with our poor resources we had to have a plan and back it, and that it was not enough to press on bull-headed, just hoping for the best.

Now I was on my own. And I felt like giving up because it didn't seem fun enough without him standing umpire at square leg or at the wickets, calling 'Over' in his l-lordly voice and signalling boundaries like a parson pronouncing benediction. But, more than anything (I realised later), having him see me at something I really knew about and him *understanding*. (Which Slingsby didn't.)

Still, I'd have chucked it up but for him (Slingsby, I mean).

He could see how it was and didn't push it. But one day he got me talking about a Test Match at Headingley when I'd seen the great Harold Larwood catapulting them down, and we got to talking about how him, the pitman, and Jardine, the gentleman, a bold determined pair, England at her best, had stuck it out in Australia in the teeth of howls there and the whines of a backbone-less M.C.C. here. . . .

Well, it's right, I thought, and we should stick it out as

120

well. I've set my hand to the plough and I'll finish the furrow. And I said as much.

'That's the spirit,' Slingsby said. 'You had us worried for a bit, that's all. Not that we don't understand—Wakerly and you having been mates for so long.'

I can't say Slingsby was a friend. Not like Wakerly. I can't even say I'd have relished a week's holiday with him even at a holiday camp. His conversation was so limited —cricket, the drapery trade and his young lady. Whereas Wakerly had a sense of fun and raised your level. And to keep up with his conversation was an effort; and this was a good thing. The New Statesman, Fascism, operatics, J. B. Priestley, anything deeper than the Methodist Recorder had been a closed book to me before.

But it was Wakerly who was dead, and there was this at least to be said for Slingsby—I understood him. Although, as I've said before, North Riding and West Riding folks are a world apart, nevertheless it has to be grudgingly admitted we talk roughly the same language. So we came to a sort of working arrangement and settled on playing off the last few games before the Rainy Season broke. Then we'd disband and wait for the Boat. Life had to go on.

But it all came back in the craziest way only a week or two later—Wakerly being gone, I mean. I was at a loose end and fished out a pile of grubby Mirrors from the rubbish box and took them back to the bed. And there she was on the front page—the beautiful blonde without shoes, the one who'd walked into the W.V.S. canteen, the spectator on the boundary. There was a big headline—

BEAUTIFUL BLONDE BLUDGEONED.
BODY FOUND IN CRICKET PAVILION.

Then it went on to say how she and a swaddy had lived out in the village cricket hut all winter, making a bed on nets and pads and cooking on an oil stove the tea-ladies used.

Until he'd killed her. It didn't say why. This face staring boldly from the past. This girl already doomed when we'd seen her, dead within a week of her silk stockinged walk in the rain.

It was an age since we'd seen her stalk insolently into that decaying canteen. Budmouth was over and Blackfen nearly over and Sinji waiting in the future. We'd glanced blindly on the boundary, unrecognising, both Wakerly and her even then with less than a twelvemonth left before the dusty pile of nets and cricket gear in a winter pavilion and the slime and ooze of a mangrove swamp.

If only you could turn back the clock! But, if you could, what could you say—'Look, it's near the finish?'

No, better you don't know: we're men and we go noisily from silence to silence.

Sixteen

You couldn't whistle up replacements on The Coast and, now, Glapthorn and I had to do the Section work between us. We coped all right without killing ourselves. (Except for aircrew there were always two men to do one job in the RAF right through the War.) The dismal thing about it was that it threw me completely on Glapthorn's company.

Although, by this time, he'd lost all his bounce from the bindings Turton had treated him to, he'd built up such a backlog of dislike that it was too late to have friends and he lived like a pariah. It boiled down to this: nobody on the Station *had* to talk to him except me. Well, anyway, I needn't have talked but I *had* to listen and, frankly, I don't think he cared so long as I was there whilst he drooled on about having been a bank cashier in civvy life and about his wife who, according to his snapshots, was a strapping blonde who lived in a fur coat and had protruding eyes.

It took a bit of working out how she'd let a specimen like Glapthorn catch her. All in all, if ever he'd got the chopper, she was the kind of woman no-one would have minded taking the sad news to and staying on to comfort her: as the song goes, she had a look of slumbrous passion. Anyway, he was missing his bouncing playmate badly. I know this because I once happened to read part of a letter he was writing. You never read such mush: most of it was frankly indecent, even if it was to his wife *and* allowing for the climate on the Coast.

But another letter I saw was from his mother. (They called him Sonny at home.) And she told him plainly that his wife was running loose with his late boss at the bank, who'd been commissioned in the Army Pay Corps and had taken her out three or four times on his last leave. She kept saying, 'and him a married man with a position, middle-aged too, with three children of his own,' as though it wouldn't have been too bad if he'd been a road-sweeping bachelor. And, when she'd reproached her, she had it thrown back in her face—'and what about their Sonny? You don't mind what he's up to, do you? You don't see nothing wrong that he's romping about out there in the sunshine with those bare black women . . .?' (It was an interesting picture.)

Well, I could always tell when he'd had a letter from home after that. He brooded for a week, and then began to sing practically all day long, every day till the next mail-boat came. It's only fair to say that he had a good voice—which he described as a light tenor. Photographic dark-rooms are as stimulating as bathrooms to songsters, and we spent an awful lot of our lives in that darkroom. It had no windows and no cracks of any kind and it was twice as tropical as anywhere else. The sweat ran down your face, under your shirt and between your fingers, till you could believe you were dissolving. Furthermore, even in U.K. I used to sweat badly, so that it was hell for me, dripping away while Glapthorn fluted away like a madman. Not being able to see him made it worse: I could *imagine* him, fishlike mouth and the ghastly moustache fluttering. For a time I, at least, believed that it was good for me until Slingsby told me that *White Horse Inn, The Belle of New York* and *The Desert Song* weren't reputable operas. 'Muck!' he said, 'just muck! You need to hear 'Uddersfield Festival Chorus in *Andel* only the once and, ever after, you can tell muck when you hear it . . .'

But, as time went on, and with Wakerly gone, I found myself getting on better with Glapthorn. The letters he was

124

receiving from his brazen wife and his fuming mother so flattened him that he just worked in a dim routine. He used to turn up at all hours of the day and night when he was off-duty and then sit and watch me in a sort of daze. Only his little parts in the Station Concert Party (Tranter's Troupe) which got up shows once a fortnight, stopped him from going right round the bend. It's remarkable how that man could sing like a bird. On the camp stage he started each appearance with such a backlog of ill-will, that it was truly amazing how he could play on that homesick mob like a virtuoso fiddler.

'Bless this house', 'Jerusalem', 'Kathleen Mavourneen', ('O why art thou silent, thou Voice of my Heart?') tugged their heart-strings left, right and centre and gave them a vision of their drab lives that never was on sea or land. Let's face it: as a songster, he was a perfectionist, this was the way he planned it. That I understood. It was the only thing I ever admired in Glapthorn—grudgingly.

Mind, he couldn't get me a-flutter, but that wasn't his fault: I'd been so worked over during evangelical revivalist weeks when I was in my teens that my emotions had jelled. You only need to be led weeping to the penitential bench once whilst the pack bays,

> 'Yes, we'll gather at the river
> The beautiful, the beautiful, the river'

and you're more or less immune from soul-rending for life.

I've said before that he used to practise in the dark-room and, as he got to know me better, he used to pull out all his stops. And the blacker the news from home came the more passionately he sang. But standing alone on the stage those Saturday nights, playing on the audience before him in the darkness, was what he lived for. From a nobody he became Somebody. The applause was like a blood transfusion to him. The rest of Tranter's Troupe made fun of him privately but they used to count on him for soothing syrup to put the lads in the despairing mood which yearned for their own Acts of Sex and Stupidity so as to block remembering.

But one day, late in the afternoon, he came into the Section half off his head and flopped onto a camera box.

'I'll not do it,' he shouted at me. 'I'll ask for a posting first.'

'What's wrong, Corporal?' I asked, taking care not to show too much interest.

'That ridiculous man has insisted I sing a duet with him next Saturday.'

'Who?'

'That stupid adjutant ass, Turton! "Watchman what of the Night." It's out of date I told him. We can't get away with that nowadays, even out here. They'd boo us off. It's too old-fashioned. "Not the way we shall do it," he says. And then—you'll not believe it—he tells me he's going to modernise it. He says I am to put on my webbing, full pack and steel helmet, and when the curtain goes up, stand in the gloom with a rifle and fixed bayonet . . .'

'A sentry,' I said.

'With a fixed bayonet! A fixed bayonet!' he repeated incredulously. 'Then he will enter wearing the Orderly Officer's armband and with pistol drawn. "You will cry 'Who goes there?' and I will answer 'Friend!' Then you will come to a smart attention and present arms and the piano will start up and I will sing (bravura), 'Watchman what of the Night? The Night of Doubting and Fear' and so on."'

He paused.

'And so on,' he repeated broodingly. 'He must be mad.'

'He can't be serious,' I said, knowing full well Turton was always deadly serious about getting his own way.

'He is, he is.' Glapthorn was about in tears. 'But I won't do it,' he said weakly. 'I'll not be made a laughing-stock. I have my reputation.'

Seventeen

But, of course, he gave in. How could he stand up to the Adjutant—especially since Turton believed he was doing him a favour and that Glapthorn *must* think it a wonderful scheme? And, then, remember Glapthorn was in a weak position, because he needed to sing; his fortnightly ten minutes of glory was something he just had to have.

But fate was against him, even after he'd surrendered. It all fell out as he'd prophesied. To begin with, he looked unbelievably unmilitary in a U.K. greatcoat and full pack —like a hunchbacked frog. When the curtain parted to disclose the wretched man cowering in the gloom, fully accoutred iu U.K. gear, there were immediate yells of 'Send the bastard overseas!' 'He knows somebody at Records!' 'Watcha guarding? The C.O.'s concubine?'

Turton himself had arranged to be spotlighted as he came on but this served only to expose his bewilderment at the hubbub. However, they struck boldly out into the arranged routine: Glapthorn presented arms like a collapsing ironmongery display and, after waiting furiously for a lull, Turton drew his revolver, brandished it and burst into, 'Watchman, what of the Night?'

Immediately, there were howls and simulated farts. I saw Glapthorn's mouth open and close two or three times, so he must have been trying to reply. The razzes, shrieks and whistles were deafening so he packed it in and cowered wretchedly before Turton, who appeared to be shouting menacingly at him as though blaming him for everything. I half thought Glapthorn was going to cry. Anyway, he was so unnerved that he stumbled, his rifle and bayonet slid away and, trying to recover them, his webbing jerked up and the full pack cascaded over his head, bringing him crashing to his knees as if he'd been shot. And wave after wave of laughing, a tide of it, swept over him. Pandemonium! Then he dragged himself up, baggage hanging round him like a bee-keeper, grabbed the rifle and began to advance and to yell and prod at Turton. What he shrieked only the Adjutant heard. Then the curtain dropped, and we saw no more. Everybody yelled 'Encore, Encore!' I did myself.

Next day he came to the Section ill and quiet. Never said a word about what had happened. Half way through the morning Turton called: he wasn't going to let him get away with it.

'The Section is scruffy this morning, Corporal. There's dust around. Surely they taught you at training school that the initial task each day is to clean the work-room.'

'Yes, sir,' said Glapthorn, looking at Turton's shoes.

'Working in the dark, it is essential that all equipment and materials should be in position. Do you agree, Corporal?'

'Yes, sir.'

'And that dust on the bromide paper, the enlarger slides and on negatives is a major contributive to scruffy reproduction?'

'Yes, sir.'

'Then get the place cleaned up, man.'

If I'd been Glapthorn, I'd have been on him like a shot, missing that last 'Corporal' and he wouldn't have had a leg to stand on. If you're an officer, you can tear as big a strip off as you like (that is if it's your own section) but you have to tear along official lines. Call your victim 'liar', 'thief', 'traitor', anything you like, but you must call him 'Corporal' too.

This persecution went on almost every day, buzzing like a dentist's drill, till Glapthorn was a bag of nerves, poor blighter, and didn't know whether he was coming or going, swaying into the battering like a man in a dream.

Until the knock-out.

It was early November and the deadline for Christmas mail home was near. I can't repeat too often that you couldn't buy anything in that hole of a town and Glapthorn, profiting from what some ex-overseas airman had told him and with his eye on a second fur coat for his wife, had brought out some low-grade bromide paper in his kitbag, like old-time traders brought beads and looking-glasses. He did an indian ink copy of the Three Wisemen on camels, a couple of palm trees, a star above and, below, 'Peace and Goodwill' printed in olde tyme lettering. Then he made a blue-print negative and began churning out photographed Christmas cards. They went like hot cakes at a bob apiece.

But it was a pity that one of his Wisemen didn't unload a little Wisdom, Glapthorn-for-the-use-of, because, when his supply of civvy paper ran out, he began to use a little and then a little more of the stuff with A. M. Crown Copyright engraved on its back.

I was staggered when I saw what he was doing. Just then, with Turton homing in for the kill, it was madness. But then, thinking back, Glapthorn *was* mad. His wife and mother and the Adjutant had pushed him over the edge.

And, one day when he had a pile of a hundred or more near the guillotine for trimming, Turton walked in and began his cold scrutiny of our activities. I was sitting near the prints and could have whipped them into a locker. But I didn't. I just moved away so as not to be associated with the racket and left them buzzing like a burglar alarm, all white and shiny, shrieking Goodwill to All Men.

'Ah,' said Turton, drawing in his breath as though he couldn't believe his luck, and he stalked across and turned a few over to make sure AIR MINISTRY PROPERTY was on the back.

I won't pile on the agony. Of course, the charge was Misappropriation of His Majesty's Property for Personal Gain and then all the usual guff about greedy profiteers jeopardising the lives of our brave merchant seamen. They stripped him to L.A.C. and would have knocked him further down the ladder to A.C.1 or A.C.2 but, after the duster episode, they didn't dare trust me with charge of the Section.

When he came back from the Court Martial, he looked ghastly; he'd met one or two erks who'd come to mock attention.

Eighteen

I never saw a man change and collapse like Corporal Glapthorn did at Sinji. Particularly after Turton got to work on him. From his high horse, stuffed with bull, to a pathetic wreck—in six months. His confidence went the same way as his wife. Perhaps she *was* his confidence. Perhaps he only reverted to what he'd been before when, to his amazement, he'd pulled her out of the raffle and began to take her for granted, and to believe it was his own transcendant worth and sterling character, which had done the trick instead of some quite inexplicable quirk which had thrown him onto her lap. I'd have known better if I'd seen her, heard her speak, watched her move. I only knew her as a pouting, furry Juno, lolling invitingly in a punt backed by cushions and reeds.

The thought of someone else bouncing around a bed with her must have been too much for him, knowing he'd never get her back. It was Wakerly and Caroline Driffield all over again—but at drain level.

'I'll be glad when this lot is over, Tom,' he told me. 'I don't want to go home—there's nothing for me there. And it's the same here—nobody likes me.'

'Oh, I wouldn't say that,' I said.

'No,' he said. 'It was the same at the Bank before I was called up. Chaps avoided me. I used to lunch on my own. But I was all right when I was with Pam. I could see other men look at her and envy me for what I'd got, and that gave me confidence. I was dead lucky to get her. It was only because my people knew hers. And then there was this

thing she had, and they wanted to feel she'd be all right . . .
Now, she's turned against me, I'm finished.'

It was about this time that he acquired the monkey.
Trader Horn had caught it in the hills, and his pals in the
billet had fastened a rope round one leg and tethered it to
a stake. They used to feed it on cook-house leavings and the
odd banana. It wasn't too wonderful a sight crouched down
in a corner, once it had given up trying to escape. It looked
like an indescribably miserable, little old man and used to
put its hands over its wizened face as though mourning its
loss of liberty. Well, in the end, it got away. Either that or
someone untied it. But, instead of fleeing back to its old
haunts, it hung around the camp just keeping out of reach.
As Wakerly would have said—it had been contaminated
by Civilisation.

Glapthorn only began to notice it when it stole some
eggs his dhobi-boy had brought him from Jassyville. He'd
left them in his topee on the table he'd made from a crate.
At first, he blamed other airmen and was very bitter about
it, but on the third day he found this monkey, sitting com-
fortably in his tent and sucking an egg. He flew into a
great rage and dashed for it, but, of course, it was away
out and along the tent ridge as he scrambled across the guy
ropes. Then it jumped into an acacia tree and he'd had it.
After that, this monkey became an obsession with him. In
fact he went so far as to lodge a complaint about it in the
Orderly Room.

'They laughed at me, the stuck-up brutes,' he said. 'I'll
show them.' So he wrote another complaint that this monkey was a menace to public health, quoting an Air Ministry
regulation and asking for its destruction as vermin and
turned this in to the M.O. 'Now those Orderly Room
clerks'll have to act,' he said.

But somebody must have got at the M.O. and told him
the monkey's side of the story; i.e. about its persecution by

Glapthorn, because this doctor, who was a bit of a joker, typed out a report to the C.O. claiming that the monkey was a valuable military asset providing the community with a 'focus for effort combative to boredom'. And the Orderly Room Sergeant, Fife, called Glapthorn in, and gleefully read it to him.

Glapthorn tried everything, even offered a reward of five bob to the dhobi-boys to catch it for him, and I heard later that he'd tried to buy drugs from the medical orderly to put it down. It became a camp joke. Corporals and sergeants would ask him how *his* monkey was, if he was going to adopt it, who the mother was, had he brought her with him, and where he kept her. . . . In fact, you might say the M.O. was right. It took our minds off the Coast, and if this M.O. had been a bit more astute he could have made his name with it. Like Boyle's Law, Pythagoras's Theorem, and this tropical boredom antidote he'd stumbled on—Glapthorn's Monkey!

But then it became ill. And the oddest thing was that, in its misery, it turned to its arch-enemy. Glapthorn found it under his bed one morning. He pulled it out and shook it. But, when it didn't struggle, he put it down again, and it just sat there. Then, I reckon he saw that his own and the monkey's plights were not dissimilar. Other erks soon noticed, gathered round and called it a poor little bugger as they watched him feed it with a syringe. For the first time, Glapthorn enjoyed a sort of popularity. But his monkey wouldn't eat and just looked mournfully out from under the little cloak and hood a rigger had made for it.

Then, one morning, Glapthorn woke up and, as usual, leaned over to look under his bed: but the monkey had rolled on its side and was dead.

That was the finish of Glapthorn. I was told that he cried and, afterwards, went and dug a hole under a palm tree near his tent, lined it with cement slabs he'd scrounged and put the monkey in a box he got from the cook house. Then he buried it.

Soon, he started going around with some crazy erks who'd been lost by Records and left on detachment on a creek. And these used to congregate at sundown round palm trees and howl. So that he was safest just sitting around, whilst I got on with it. He used to stand up when Turton came in, but I feel pretty sure he hadn't a clue what the swine was binding on about.

Then he broke up completely, and they took him into sick quarters and kept him there until he was repatriated. In fact I only saw him once again—staring from a window, stroking his bald head (and occasionally howling).

They sent another corporal from Command: I forget his name.

Nineteen

The last but one game of my campaign was already fixed—against the Liberator Squadron. The Semi-Final you might call it, because, if we lost there really wasn't much point in playing the Station XI.

This game, the Liberator Squadron one, is worth telling about because from it sprang all the later trouble. So this is what happened. Slingsby and I could never pick a side until the last minute because of bods being wanted for duty, and I was in the Section one morning when the C.O. came round on one of his snap inspections. He never really looked at things, but I suppose he felt he ought to be seen now and then.

'Ah,' he said, 'Aircraftsman Flanders! Flanders, I've been hearing about your cricket side. You've been doing jolly well. Yes, jolly well. I'm very pleased that you fellows have organised some recreation. Far too many nowadays wait for someone to entertain them. Yes, jolly good! Playing the Liberator crowd too I hear?'

'Yes, sir.'

'Ah, good! Yes, well, there's a couple of my officers would like a game. You can find places for them? Both tell me they played for their schools. 1st XI men. Now, can you manage that, Flanders?'

You couldn't hum and haw with your C.O. A wink is as good as a kick from him.

'Yes, sir,' I said as cheerfully as I could manage.

'Good man, good man! Mr. Oates—I think you'll find

him a jolly useful bat. And the Adjutant. You know him of course. Good! I trust you'll lick them, Flanders.'

And off he went, walking-stick and all, saying 'Jolly good!'

I looked around for Wakerly to laugh. It had been the sort of scene he delighted in. Then I went to break the news to Slingsby.

We felt the depressing effect of this soon enough in the shape of a verbal message to Slingsby (not me) by an Orderly Room toady—'The Adj. says you all have to wear shirts in the game tomorrow . . .' (Of course, in that climate, as soon as we airmen were off duty, we stripped down to the waist, wearing only shorts and pumps.) Wearing the shirts against our normal custom wasn't too bad: it was the irritation of him wedging himself into the side and then interfering. But there was no getting out of it, and we wore them.

I won the toss and batted. I'd never found a competent partner, so I put the new officer, Oates, in Number Two. He was a dead loss—dollied up a catch the fourth ball of the first over, having nearly run me out on the third. But their bowling was very plain, straight up and down stuff and, though the other wickets fell regularly, I stayed and made my biggest score (in Africa)—124 not out, and we declared at 201 for 8. (Well, if I don't say it nobody else will—it was a concert performance; my timing was dead-on and the last fifty came in twenty-five minutes. In fact, I scored 18 in the last over and ended the innings by hammering a ball only just short of a length round over long-leg. It went like a rocket, a six, struck high up on the trunk of a palm tree and bounced back like a golf ball and hit a spectator. You only get a dozen innings like that in twenty years' batting.)

Neither Slingsby nor Trader was in form though, and when one of the Liberator sergeants, a thickset man with a black moustache, and an airman called Hawke-Jones got set, the runs kept coming at an uncomfortably steady pace until they were 175 for 7 and no sign of the partnership breaking. Then I panicked and, instead of trusting my side, I switched myself into fielding positions where I imagined the catches were likely to go. So I wasn't controlling the game any more—just being pushed along by the current of events.

Then Turton shouted across to me, 'Flanders, I should like an over.' Frankly, I'd forgotten him. He was up to his Budmouth antics, of course; he *had* to be different. The best he could do here was to tie knots in the four corners of a handkerchief, like farm-labourers at home sometimes did, and to wear it as a sun-hat.

'Next over, then,' I said.

I know I shouldn't have done. A captain should let no-one dictate to him on the field. That I did was a measure of the flap I'd got myself into.

And the impossible happened. In the first over he clean bowled the sergeant and the incoming batsman and, an over later, finished off the side. Just plain straight balls such as Slingsby, Stone and Trader had been belting down all afternoon.

As we walked off, Slingsby looked across at me. 'Jam!' he said.

The new officer stopped. 'Thanks for the game, Flanders,' he said. 'Sorry I didn't help much.'

Turton, of course, just *left*. Full stop!

So there we were. One more game and we'd be there. Everything had worked out to plan. Slingsby must have suddenly guessed what was passing through my mind because he suddenly began to bawl,

' "One more river and that's the River of Jordan,
One more river, there's just one more river to cross." '

Slingsby singing! It must be his nerves, I thought. So I wasn't the only one who'd panicked? Good!

Twenty

The old hands had told us what the Rains were like, how you never were really dry, how your shoes went green and the mosquitoes multiplied. So I drew a deep breath, as you might say, and fixed a date for the last game. It had been a long, long trail from that first nervous match against the Stores Section.

For my liking, there was a lot too much interest in this last match. Our being unbeaten had been noticed at last and it got around that this final victory over the Rest of the Station was what we'd been working towards. There was a lot of speculation in the billets and a fair amount of betting, with the odds, naturally, very much against us. Plainly, it had caught everyone by surprise, this quiet little campaign working itself out unnoticed. Men I scarcely knew, N.C.O.s and one or two squadron officers, stopped to discuss the chances. Even the posting of the Commanding Officer and arrival of a new one didn't catch their interest more. And, in the billet, I saw erks taking a quick look as though they'd never seen me before. I had to take a grip on myself.

But it worried me even more when Slingsby came to tell me about Trader Horn.

'He's not looking too well,' he said. 'He looks washed out. I've asked his mates and they say he's a dead loss on the job. Just sits around and sleeps if they give him half a chance. As soon as he's off duty, he slips off in his canoe. Except nowadays he doesn't bring bananas back. He just comes back more on his knees than when he sets off. He's going to let us down; you can see that a mile off.'

Well, this is a poor look-out, I thought. I must have made it crystal-clear that, if I couldn't get runs and if Trader couldn't winkle out their best bats, we'd had it against a really good side. In fact, we were on the razor edge all the time. Wood and Stone could stay in but neither was capable of scoring more than a dozen and, as a rule, Slingsby could only get rid of anyone who didn't play the bowling according to its merits. If we were going to beat the Station or even make a game of it, I had to make a really big score and Trader had to rip out their openers.

'I'll have a word with him,' I said.

And I did. And all I got was evasion. He even looked worse than he'd been described, big bags under his eyes, thin as a rake, in fact his hair was coming out.

'I'm all right,' he kept saying. 'Absolutely fit.'

'Are you on the booze?' I asked him.

'Can't afford it,' he said.

'Worried about something? At home I mean.'

'Home! I wouldn't care if I never saw it again. I like it here. If there's anything worrying me, it's *going* home. . . .' Then he went off.

That gave me something to think about: he must have been the only type at Sinji who wasn't dreaming, Roll on the Boat. In fact, I doubt if there was another anywhere else in the world on Overseas like him. He was unique.

It's something to do with his canoe trips, I thought, and I fixed with Slingsby to watch out for Trader after chop. Then, keeping our distance, we let him go down to the Creek and paddle to the first bend. Then we shot into the M.B.C. dinghy I'd borrowed and, taking an oar apiece, rowed after him.

We let him keep one bend ahead until he reached the river's main channel which was two or three hundred yards wide. Then we had to let him go on but, as he was heading straight for a low island—well, scarcely an island, more of a sandbank—we didn't worry too much. He pulled his canoe onto the beach pretty quick and marched off into a little stockade made of driftwood and flattened oil drums.

If it hadn't been for the approaching Game, what we found would have been funny. In the shadow of a wicker and daub hut, lying on a RAF bed, was Trader. Behind him a well-developed negress was fanning him with a contraption of dried palm leaves and a second woman was holding some kind of drink in a beer bottle. Neither was wearing a stitch and, when they saw us, twittered like birds, ran round the hut and into it.

I'll say this for Trader: true to his great quality as a bowler, he didn't turn a hair. But Slingsby was scandalised and began lecturing him like somebody from Greyfriars Annual.

'Oh belt up,' Trader said. 'And grow up.' He lowered his feet and shouted in African. The two women, followed by two or three kids, came sidling round the hut with a bottle apiece. They'd wrapped some window curtaining round themselves and one of them picked up a palm leaf and went on ventilating where she'd left off.

It turned out, according to Trader, that in those parts, when a woman is widowed she becomes the servant of a brother-in-law or whoever of her late husband's family gives her a billet. Women are so plentiful that no-one will marry her. Trader had found these two and their children just about starving, living rough in the town and he'd got them out here and was keeping them on his pay-roll for services rendered. Well, you could see they thought of him as a Fount of Blessings and it was plain there was no lack of enthusiasm in keeping up their side of the arrangement. He'd promised that, when he was posted home, he'd give them ten quid apiece to tide them over and get them back to their village up near the border. No deception about it; just a pure piece of concubinage.

Well, this was all very interesting, but to admire his humanity and initiative wasn't what we'd come to do. And I knew it was no use appealing to him or arguing the toss.

'Trader,' I said, 'you're jigging yourself into the ground. Tell these young ladies that you're going on seven days leave. (He began to protest.) If you come near this island or them until after the Game, I'll spread it around camp and your life won't be worth living. And if S.H.Q. hears, you'll be posted down to Sierra Leone or up to the Pointe. No kidding. And Slingsby and I will be checking where you are all hours of the day and night until then. After that, you can kill yourself in peace.'

He took it very well: he knew I meant it all right. We shook hands on it, and then he took us for a stroll round his island. The hut walls were papered with pages of Picture Post, chiefly showing The Royal Family. Apparently, they all kipped in together. Except for the hut and the stockade which had been there when Trader had bought it from a couple of fishermen, there was nothing except a driftwood branch stuck like a flagpole on a spit at the end of the island. It had a filthy rag hanging from it and there was a couple of fish and a corned-beef-issue tin a quarter full lying at its foot.

'It's their juju,' he explained. 'Holy ground. The fishes and stuff are for the spirit they claim lives here and keeps an eye on things while I'm back at Sinji.'

Slingsby wanted to begin a big argument about this. He was scandalised by everything, first the women and then the heathen practices. But I took him off and he didn't speak until we reached the camp again.

'It mightn't have been so bad,' he said, 'if he'd only had *one* woman.'

We tied up the boat and walked back to the billets.

'Look,' I said, 'we've got to decide. What about Turton and Oates? Do we pick 'em or don't we?'

'We'll have to pick the Adj,' Slingsby said. 'After all there's no getting away from it: it was the wickets he took in the Liberator game that pulled the fat out of the fire.'

'Yes,' I said, 'but do we *have* to? A committee doesn't *have* to pick anybody. I mean, wasn't that the whole point of us making it A 697 Squadron XI not *The* XI? Frankly, having him around put me off. I don't think we ever should have got into that mess for him to pull us out of, if we'd been on our own.'

Slingsby considered this.

'Well,' he said in his flat West Riding voice, 'he won't like it if we don't choose him. Let's ask Woody. Then, if Turton or anyone else starts cribbing, we can say it was a committee decision made "after considering all aspects of the situation" (which sounds well and means nothing).'

So we asked little Wood and he didn't seem to need any time at all to settle it. 'Don't pick him, Tom. It's not the same when he's playing.'

'All right,' I said. 'Then what about F/O Oates?'

'Not worth his place,' said Slingsby.

'Same here,' said Wood.

So we picked the same side that had got us so far. And pinned it up.

Twenty-One

I had worked it out that, once the breeze began to blow in from the west—that is across the mangrove swamps from the sea—it would stay in that quarter and would win the game for us. Trader, with his high left-arm action, bowling from the Guard Room end would use it to float the ball to-wards the slips, and their batsmen would follow it round and tickle it into Slingsby's big hands. And Slingsby him-self, from the Work Area end, with the palm trees masking the ball, would jerk his fast off-breaks into their bodies and I'd be waiting at silly-mid-on. It was a blessed breeze.

I borrowed a timber frame from Ground Defence [from which they used to hang a bag of straw to practise bayonet plunging] and I fitted this up across the popping crease. Then I chalked a cross chest high on the sack and, after work, set on Trader and Slingsby bowling short to lift the ball. And, out of the corner of my eye, I saw Maidstone and Fife stop to watch. I knew it would worry them, because find me the batsman who likes the ball up at him, especially when it's moving in or away. We packed it in then because it had been for their benefit, not Trader's nor Slingsby's, that I set the thing up.

The day before the game the breeze still blew. If any-thing, it had veered a couple of points and was coming in from forward short-leg towards gulley which was better than I'd dared hope, putting a sharper drag on off-breaks and carrying the outswingers with a keener nip from the matting. As I've said before, I like working to a plan: it gives you that extra confidence in a panic. Of course, you never can rule out luck in any game, cricket more than most, but it's plain madness to bank on it.

That week, most of the Catalinas were away on dispersal so that we were slack in the section and I was sitting under our mango tree getting the benefit of the breeze, feeling a bit weak at the knees thinking about this final game. I felt sure that the Station XI were so damned confident of winning that *their* only plan would be simplicity itself—get rid of me and then massacre the others. It was a great responsibility.

I was pondering the horrors of being out first ball or first over, and all my careful plans over the past months collapsing like a pack of cards into a ridiculous heap, when Slingsby came.

I could see he was blazing mad; he was so pale.

'Turton's made himself captain,' he said, his voice trembling.

I was staggered. Then I went cold and I began to shake in all my limbs: something I can never remember happening before. Outside old time history books, I couldn't even begin to imagine anything like this happening.

'He can't,' I said. 'It's our team. It isn't *his* team.'

'Not according to him. He's called it *The* 697 Squadron XI.'

He hurried me off to the board outside the squadron offices.

The full force of what he'd done didn't hit me until I saw his name heading the list and my own near the bottom, and a Squadron Ldr. Rumm I'd never heard of—a new flight commander it turned out—and saw that Henty and Cork had been pushed out, both only run-of-the-mill players who couldn't be relied on to score ten between them and only really able to stop the ball with their legs. But loyal lads who'd come all the way up with us.

'Ah, Flanders, looking over the Team?' Turton had come up behind us. I could think of nothing to say: I felt stunned. 'After the way you let things get out of hand in the Liberator Game, it was thought in the Mess that I'd better run things,' he said. 'Quite a strong side. If we all pull our weight we should give them a good game.'

I still could only stare stupidly at the board and Slingsby at his feet as he walked off. Oddly enough, in the middle of this horror, I thought what a tactical blunder he'd made putting Slingsby No. 8 and replacing Wood as vice-captain by one of the officers. There was always a chance they might have deserted me but, now he'd given them a back-hander apiece, they weren't likely to forgive him any more than I was.

But 'Ah, Flanders, it was thought in the Mess that I'd better run things . . .' I'll hear it till my dying day and still feel the baffling heat of the squadron street and my own coldness. It was like a scene from a Western. He'd done it! Usurped our weeks of work and planning just like that! He had all the authority and power he could use, but he had to take over our little corner too! Damn and blast him!

By next morning, I'd settled into depression. There didn't seem to be a thing that I could do about this abominable business. In the day-to-day routine of service life, you had to suffer fools and put up with rations of inhumanity from N.C.Os. and officers without answering back. But interference with leisure—that was something new. I'll be frank: I didn't care now if we lost or won. This wasn't the Game we'd been planning and preparing for, the Game that made sense of all the other games we'd won. I've spoken of this before so I'll not labour it.

But, even so, I'd have gone on and played the game, shelving all responsibility of course, but played as I always played, if it hadn't been for the S.H.Q. Sergeant, Fife. I was sitting just inside the Section door, when he poked his head in and said, 'Ready for the thrashing we're going to give you Thursday, Flanders?'

'You'll not be giving *me* one,' I said. 'I'm not captain and it's not my team.' But he laughed and went off laughing. And you could tell from the attitude of his cronies that it was me they had it in for, to smash *my* side and put *me* in my place amongst the fragments. Little Wood put it into words. 'They're going to crucify us,' he said. That was pitching it a bit thick; I don't care for scriptural words taken from their setting.

I half-heartedly tried to persuade the temporary corporal to insist that I couldn't be spared from duty on Thursday, but he had his ear close to the ground and knew what was going on. Only a sharp bout of malaria could save me from the bitterest pill I'd ever had to swallow. One or two of the lads and Slingsby came round to the billet but, honestly, I couldn't bring myself to talk about it. I still felt numb.

And, when it came to the afternoon itself, I didn't know where to put myself. As skipper, there'd been so much to see to—last minute tactical arguments with Slingsby, jollying up the nervous ones, screwing up my own will to win as I took the over-elaborate pains with my kit I always indulged in (because you have to *think* the game before you play it). It was awful not going out to toss with Maidstone, just waiting to be told what it was to be, bat or field. As it turned out it was *field*—Turton had won the toss and put them in. (That showed how little confidence he had in us!)

Maidstone opened for them and, after he'd been missed by Turton in the slips (where Slingsby should have been) in Trader's first over, they never looked back. Trader and Slingsby were good bowlers; in fact very good. But on asphalt, accuracy wasn't enough. I don't want to appear immodest, but they needed me to direct their fire-power from mid-off and he'd stuck me third man and long-on so that the refinements of the game (if there were any) were lost to me.

About the tenth over, remembering his success against the Liberator Squadron, he put himself on at one end and the new officer, Rumm, at the other. But, as anybody who understood the game could see, Maidstone and Co. with their tails up were a very different kettle of fish, and they put the pair of them to the sword, Maidstone particularly taking anything over-pitched and thumping it like a cannonball through the covers and making massive pulls out of short balls. It was butchery.

I won't prolong the agonizing details—they hurt me still. It was enough to see Slingsby looking half crazy, furiously pushing his long forelock back over his brow, or to have to listen to their supporters making as much row as a cup-tie. The Station side really stuck it in deep and then twisted. At half-past five they declared at 217 for 3.

'Christ!' Stone said, and put his head in his hands and rocked to and fro in misery on the bench under the acacia trees.

'Well, chaps,' Turton said in his jerky way, 'it's a lot. But, if they got 'em, so can we.'

He pinned up the batting order. S/Ldr. Rumm and F/O Oates numbers one and two, then Stone, then myself, Wood, Turton himself, Slingsby and so on. We didn't talk much as we sat there waiting. As a matter of fact, I was feeling pretty normal up till then, nothing like as nervous as I usually was. It was Fife and what he said that sent the balloon up. The Station went out, tossing the ball around one to the other and laughing but *he* couldn't resist rubbing it in to pay off old scores. He paused by the bench where I was sitting with Wood and Slingsby. 'Take your beating like a man, Flanders,' he said. Only the three of us heard him. The man was a sadist.

I didn't say anything. This is important because of what

came afterwards. I didn't need to as I glimpsed the faces of the other two as they glared at his back.

But he could laugh all right; second ball of the first over down went Rumm's bailliwick. He'd missed one of Angus's and that usually was fatal. Oates didn't last much longer, and it was two wickets for three runs when I went in, and, then, when poor Stone had been caught at point, it was three for five. Wood came waddling in (he was slightly bow-legged) and began to drop his bat like a hen-house shutter, even though Fife, bowling really fast, soon nipped his fingers. It was no joke. Then the poor kid was hit again and his hands began to run blood. I'd tried to get him out of the habit but, this time, he forgot all I'd told him. Let's face it: he didn't know how to lift his bat *and* stay in. And Fife knew his limitations and bowled at them.

But Wood gritted his teeth (I heard him!) and stuck it out. And, watching him from the other end, I felt (as you might say) a sudden lightening of the spirit. I nearly laughed aloud. What it amounted to was that this back-street London kid who'd learnt his cricket in an elementary school playground had swallowed my pep talks over the past two months and was carrying them out mechanically. It made me suddenly ashamed too. So when this awful over stopped and he was wringing his bloody fingers, I called gently, 'Good lad, Woody!' and winked at him and he must have got the message when I lowered my stance and then let everything more than three inches wide of the off stump go through to the wicket-keeper. After that, I only tried to score a single an over just to keep him from the chopping block.

You might say that this was the crisis of the match. In ten overs we scored but eight runs. And suddenly Turton stood up, cupped his hands and yelled, 'Get a move on, Flanders.' I didn't look directly at him, because I could see the other lads sitting up looking cheerful for the first time with Slingsby jumping up and down behind them. Next over, Wood missed one and was lbw and in came Turton. He glared down the pitch at me and called sharply, 'We'll have some quick singles.' And, in fact, he glanced his very first ball gracefully to leg, his favourite shot I suppose, and came racing down at me. 'Come on, come on, man,' he shouted. I didn't move and he reached my end, stuck his face no more than a foot from mine and yelled like a maniac, 'What the hell are you playing at, Flanders!' But Maidstone had moved quietly round from the slips to short fine-leg and the ball had gone straight into his hands.

The silence was electric. Turton suddenly knew something had gone wrong. He looked round and saw the ball being tossed gently into the air. 'I'm afraid you're out, sir,' the umpire said.

The Station still kept at it. With five wickets down, I suppose they still thought they had a half chance of winning. But they must have seen the writing on the wall when Slingsby came in and began to smother everything. He more or less sat astride his bat as though he'd taken up permanent residence in the crease. It was growing dark by now and Fife had just about lost control of himself, so that I heard Maidstone say quietly to him, 'Steady on, man, you'll kill somebody.'

Then Turton intervened for the last time. He advanced a few yards on to the field of play and called, 'Flanders, you are to retire.'

I didn't shift and he called again. The game just stopped. But I know the rules. A captain can make an entire side declare, but he can't winkle out one player. It would have been fatal to have argued this out with him though. So I didn't look at him and stayed put and took my guard.

'Play on,' said the umpire, and Maidstone gave me a shy grin. Slingsby got a glancing blow on his head and, after that, didn't know whether he was coming or going and just went through the motions as taught in Ossett and District. Ten minutes later, you could hardly see who was in the long-field or even at extra cover and every third ball I was being rattled in the ribs. But we wouldn't appeal against the light.

Then, all at once, the game stopped. The umpires looked at one another and lifted the bails. And that was an end to it. It was crazy and silly and funny. 217 for 3 them, 27 for 5 us. A draw!

Twenty-Two

Unfortunately, there were no dark-room jobs for me when Fife came officiously next afternoon to say that the Station Sports Council had been convened to investigate my Unsporting Conduct.

'Well, he can't come,' the new corporal said, 'I want him here. He has too much time off for cricket. And next time, when you want one of my Section, Sergeant, you should come to me first. You'd be on me fast enough if I came round to S.H.Q. and took one of *your* men.'

'He's wanted by the Station Sports Council,' Fife said stiffly but I could see it had shaken him. Going above the head of a section head was walking on very thin ice. (I knew a case where an operations officer with an urgent signal to despatch found a teleprinter operator asleep with the job undone, and getting into a fearful row because he tore a strip off her there and then in his rightful rage, instead of reporting her to her section commander.)

'Anything to do with sport can wait till he's off duty,' the corporal said.

'Right, Corporal, and I'll report your unco-operative attitude to the Committee.' He glared menacingly at me and went off with long furious strides. Those S.H.Q. brutes had me on the hook and they weren't going to let me go.

After that, the corporal was as jumpy as me. He fiddled around with some forms he'd already completed, and I dusted the enlarger I'd finished when I first came on duty. We weren't kept waiting long. Turton fairly shot in (wearing his topee).

'Flanders,' he snapped, 'report to the Sports Council immediately.'

I stood to attention, put on my topee, saluted and, as I went, I heard him give my would-be protector a parting blast.

The Council was sitting around a table covered with a blanket. Everybody looked judicial except Maidstone, the Station skipper, who was examining the back of his hands with great attention.

There was no chair for me and I was left standing before them, which made it clear that I'd been tried and sentenced and my presence was only necessary for the execution. The Chairman, F/O Ruskin, called on Turton to give his report. He told them what he'd shouted at me after the game, that I'd gone over his head and ordered the lads to wreck the game by not trying to win. It was too incredible for words. I could understand him going on like that in the heat of the game, but to still talk about playing to win with two hundred and eighteen runs to get in an hour and a half left in the last of the light! Mr. Ridd, at Budmouth, had been dead right: he simply didn't understand cricket.

I looked as dumb as I could and tried to stay at attention and fixed my gaze on the wall just above the Chairman's head, and set about letting them get the very minimum satisfaction out of the operation.

Then he called on Maidstone: the idea was to get unbiased confirmation I suppose. He began to mumble.

'Speak up, Maidstone,' Ruskin said, but no-one could make sense of the poor fellow's blathering, except that it was clear he wanted no part in the business. So Ruskin asked sharply,

'Did you form the impression that A.C.2 Flanders was deliberately trying to make it a drawn game?'

'Yes,' said Maidstone, 'but when you consider—'

'Did you think he was deliberately not trying to score runs?'

'The bowling was quite accurate—'

'That isn't an answer.'

'I think he knew they couldn't get them,' said Maidstone, 'so he didn't kill himself over the job.'

'In your opinion could he have scored more quickly?' Turton said sharply.

'The light wasn't getting any better,' Maidstone answered unhelpfully, still staring at the table top.

The Chairman must have decided that this was all he was going to get from him, so he turned to the Adjutant. 'Now F/Lt. Turton,' he said, 'in your opinion did Flanders deliberately usurp your authority as captain and persuade some of your squadron's side to make the game a fiasco?'

'Certainly he did. But for him the rest of the airmen would have played a good sporting game, win or lose. In short, they would have played Cricket. It was self evident that he meant to sabotage the game from the minute he went in. Furthermore, he deliberately disobeyed several orders. At one point I ordered him to get a move on. And finally, as you know, I took the unprecedented step of going on to the field and insisting that he must retire.'

'And he refused?'

'He didn't answer, so I said, "Flanders, did you hear what I have just said?"'

'And what did he say?'

'He said, Yes, he had heard me.'

'And what happened then?'

'The umpire asked me to leave the playing area.'

'I didn't mean that,' Ruskin said hastily. 'I mean, did he retire?'

'He did not. And I want it to be put on record that I am bitterly ashamed for my side, and I here and now concede victory to the Station XI.'

'Thank you, sir,' said the creeper, Fife.

There was a longish pause. I suppose they thought to unnerve me. As a matter of fact, it just came across me what a kids' game it was. I was reminded of those absurd meetings of holy prefects in boarding school stories. Anyway, once a game's over, you can't change its result. And *that* game was drawn, yea even unto the end of Time.

At last Ruskin said, 'Well, Flanders, you have heard everything, what have you to say?'

I knew they were only waiting for a chance to jump down my throat, so I said, 'Nothing, sir.'

'Do you admit that what F/Lt. Turton has told us is true?'

'No, sir.'

'Oh,' shouted the Adjutant. 'Are you accusing me of falsehood?'

I didn't answer that and there was another silence.

'Please explain yourself,' said Ruskin.

'I didn't persuade the others to do anything.'

'You deny you said anything to them?'

'No, I don't deny that I said to L.A.C. Slingsby and Air-craftsman Wood that I proposed to take a ...'

'We should like your exact words.'

'I said they'd only beat us over my body, I think.'

'And that was enough?'

I didn't answer.

'And that was enough?' Turton yelled.

'Yes,' I said.

'Were you annoyed because you weren't Captain?' Fife sneered.

I wasn't going to fall into that one and decided a bit of hypocrisy wouldn't be out of place.

'No,' I said. 'It wasn't *my* team.'

'What do you mean—it wasn't *your* team?' said the Adjutant.

155

'It was 697 Squadron 1st XI,' I said. 'My team used to be A 697 Squadron XI. L.A.C. Slingsby was the Secretary and I was the Captain.'

'Were you elected?' he jeered.

'No,' I said.

'Then who made you Captain?'

'I made myself.'

All except Maidstone began to laugh.

I realised I was playing it their way, so I shut up. They went binding on some more about Sportsmanship, Cricket being more than a Game, how it had shaped our Nation, etcetera, etcetera . . . and then told me to wait outside for their decision.

When they called me in again, they said that they were utterly disgusted and had decided, in the interests of good sportsmanship at Sinji, that I was a quite unsuitable person and hoped that I would have the decency not to play any more cricket whilst I was there.

So I came to attention, saluted and left.

Twenty-Three

So he'd won. He'd beaten me as he'd beaten Wakerly and Glapthorn. He'd taken away from all of us what we wanted most. Glapthorn's self esteem, Wakerly's Caroline and from me the only thing that had made Sinji tick for me. And, one after one, we'd let him. Well, as far as he knew, I'd only half let him. But I knew. I'd built up that team to *win* that last Game, not to stop the other side winning.

It was no use moaning about it; it would have got me nowhere. Even if the Station would have given us a return fixture, I wouldn't want to have played in it; he'd spoilt it. I didn't want to touch a bat again on that coast. We had a meeting about it and I put forward my views. I felt too humiliated to tell them what had happened when they'd had me before the Council. I just said, 'Well, lads, we had a good run for our money. It was a bit of fun while it lasted.' I told them how I'd appreciated their support, and how we would laugh in years to come about some of those games we'd played on that baked mud-patch, that it was a pity that it had to end as it did, that it wasn't our fault and there'd been nothing we could have done about it, blah, blah, blah. . . .

'But we weren't beat,' Wood said, holding up his bandaged hands.

'Well, you're maybe right, Tom,' Slingsby said. 'I don't think we could get Trader to play again anyway. He's had cricket.'

The thought of Trader making up for lost time on his sandbar tickled me.

'When the War is over, I bet he'll come back,' I said. 'He'll probably be able to buy Sinji, hangars, cookhouse and the lot for a fiver if the bush hasn't swallowed it. And he'll set up his H.Q. in the Officers' Mess and, of an evening, exercise his wives by making them field for him, a stumper and *three* long-stops. ['And in 2,000 A.D., anthropologists will f-find a new tribe with a Fertility Dance exactly twenty-two yards long. With a Freudian t-terminology—maidens, b-balls, no-balls and bum-balls' . . . I heard Wakerly inside my head.]

I picked up my mug and set off for the cookhouse. It was about the time of day they put out a couple of buckets of Liberian green coffee. Young Wood caught up with me.

'You know, Tom,' he said, 'I'll remember that innings as long as I live. I don't care if I never play again, because I'll never play in another game of cricket like that last one. Maybe we didn't win, but it was the best game we had. Half of it, anyway.'

'*He* beat us,' I said.

But he stopped and caught my arm.

'He didn't. No, he didn't. You didn't hear him raving up and down the boundary like we did. Look how he came out and yelled at you to give in. And you didn't. All of us knew then we'd stopped playing Maidstone and even Fife and their crowd, and that the seven of us were playing *him*. And we beat him.'

He stopped and looked startled at his own p-perspicacity (as Wakerly would have said).

It's a point, I thought. Maybe you're right. But I didn't agree or disagree with him. Anyway, I couldn't give my full attention to the idea because, when we got to the cookhouse, something was stirring. There was a lot of infuriated shouting going on about the so-called chop they were dishing up for supper. Chop was always fairly awful at Sinji, but that was to be expected; and those of us who'd made it when the

158

Mungo Park went down knew all about transport problems. But, about this time, things had become really grim. The canned spuds were grey and dished up like cement beginning to jell. And there was something terribly wrong with the meat when you got it. They said that it was from a boat bound for the prison colony on the Andamans that had put in down south near Freetown, given up the struggle and quietly foundered, so they had to unload the cargo and feed it to us troops. In the War nothing, as you will recall, had to be wasted.

There'd been one or two isolated complaints to the Adjutant but they got the good old perennial about our brave merchant seamen and having to tighten our belts etc. This wasn't helped by reports from mess-wallahs that things were much better for the officers and sergeants over on the other side of the parade ground. Even so, Turton might have got away with it but for the M.B.C. Now these were a queer lot, failed aircrew [not through lack of courage but of brains], and most of them were upper class chaps from the same kind of school or better than the officers. Anyway, you'll have gathered that, once they began to boil, they weren't the sort to sit down under Turton's brand of patriotic wish-wash.

When we got inside, they were banging their irons and playing hell with the cooks, shouting they wouldn't eat garbage. The Cookhouse Sergeant was on his way down through all the motions from bellowing threats to pleading it was no fault of his. Then, when he saw he wasn't getting anywhere, he muttered something to one of his corporals, who slipped off and came back with Turton and the Guardroom Sergeant (who looked pretty sheepish because some of his own men had to eat this same horrible chop).

Hearing the din as he approached must have given Turton time to weigh up the situation, because he went straight to the counter and held up a hand. When the din died, he said crisply, 'There is only one way to make a complaint that I know or the Royal Airforce Manual knows. And that is to put it in writing to your Commanding Officer. That is what you must do.'

It sounded so reasonable and sensible to everyone who hadn't got him weighed up. There was a bit of resentful muttering and then the erks ate what they could and the M.B.C. wallahs went off to their quarters, drafted a complaint and asked to see the C.O.

Well, this of course was a scene Turton could play backwards with his eyes shut. *He* received the deputation and before they'd time to open their mouths, harangued them that he took more than a dim view of this, that he took a most serious exception to it, indeed, that it was nothing more than going behind his, the Adjutant's back, that it was nothing but irresponsible trouble-making by a few malcontents, that it was his duty to screen his Commanding Officer from trivial complaints. . . .

Then he ordered them out and, of course, did nothing about it—except maybe to rub his hands.

But he wasn't dealing with Glapthorn now. These M.B.C. crews were resourceful characters and not easily put down and, soon, there were rumours of a strike going the rounds amongst tradesmen who used M.B.C. boats to get out to the Trot. And this call to action spread to the more skilled trades like the instrument-bashers who, mostly, were grammar school old-boys and well read in the annals of civil strife.

So, one morning (I almost said 'one fine morning' but all Sinji mornings were sickeningly fine), instead of parading for work, the entire M.B.C. reported sick, complaining of Malnutrition and Lack of Sustenance. So all maintenance work came to a full-stop. It was all very exciting and near to mutiny I suppose, but it brought Turton on the run to the cookhouse to inspect the chop and give it a certificate. But, no sooner did he show his long nose than the erks really

160

went over the top and began banging their dishes on the tabletops and chanting, 'Bugger off you bastard! [I hate foul language but that is what they said.] Bring out the new C.O.!' He went deathly pale and retreated.

He must have panicked badly, because he did fetch the C.O. But the cooks, to save their own miserable skins, had opened up their secret hoards and served big helpings of choice morsels whilst the Wingco was inspecting the hatch. Naturally, he saw nothing to complain of and, looking mad, marched off muttering something that boded ill for the M.B.C. Then the old chop came out and, when we began to yell again, the cooks grinned and dropped the hatches to shut us off.

But one stalwart, a corporal who had remustered from the Navy, turned the tide of battle with one bold, determined stroke. Brilliant! As carefully as a detective files finger-prints, he wrapped up both his plate and its moribund burden in a copy of the *Daily Mirror* and, insisting on his undoubted rights—won by Magna Carta etc. as a freeborn Englishman—to see his Commanding Officer, unwrapped the grisly evidence as a witness to cry forth for justice (like the stones).

'What is this shit?' cried the C.O. (He had just completed a terrifying spell in Beaus, diving through showers of it at Jerry convoys in the Skag, and still spoke in basic English.)

'This is my tiffin, Sir—(M.B.C. wallahs, wherever possible, used Indian Army commissioned vocabulary)—We've been fed muck like this for a month or more.'

'Then send for the Adjutant—one time.'

When one officer savages another, you don't get a round-by-round commentary: they have to keep up appearances before the coolies. And I'd never have known but for listening in on one of Pouncey-Pinkney's curtain chats. It probably was meant for me, anyway.

('I had a frightful experience this a.m., dear boy. Quite distasteful. I happened to be recuperating from attempted rape under the C.O.'s window while he had that disgusting man, Turton, on the carpet. Afterwards they had to send it to the dry-cleaners.' 'It? Turton?' asked Pinkney. 'The carpet?')

The New Man had weighed up the situation pretty well it seemed. Evidently an increasing number of officers detested Turton who had put things across them by using the late C.O.'s authority, and they had found ways of indicating to the New Man that to chop him down to size would be a very popular move. And the tiffin arrived in its parcel at exactly the right time. This C.O., with his nerves still shrieking from flak in the Skag, must have made a very thorough job of it, because when I next saw Turton he looked as though he'd been felled with a hedge-stake. He came into the Section and I don't think he saw me: as much as anything, he reminded me of Glapthorn in decline. His boss must have enjoyed his first go so much that he repeated the goring daily. And one or two others in the Mess, with scores to pay off, may have been trampling too.

Well, Old Sport, I thought, You've got what was coming at long last. I'm only sorry Wakerly can't see you. Even Glapthorn. It only shows I was right; it's but a matter of hanging on.

But this couldn't do any of the three of us any good now. It had happened too late.

About a week after this blew up, I was coming away from the Working Area in the middle of the afternoon and, when I came round the bend, I almost ran into Turton. He was standing in the roadway as if he was out on his feet, pole-axed but still standing. It was like Glapthorn used to stand and the Lost Men from Down the Coast howling under their tree. And this was the same place (within a yard or two)

162

where we'd first met again at Sinji, the place where he'd humiliated me. You have to remember this.

I wondered if he was going to stop me and try it on again, so I looked swiftly over my shoulder: the road was empty.

Well, I thought, The game's turned as games always do. It's you that's back-pedalling now. It's you that's on the good old slippery slope, not Glapthorn, not Wakerly, not me. And you're not going to push yourself back by treading me down. . . .

And this is exactly what happened: I'd read his mind completely. It was like seeing a film again in slow motion.

'Flanders,' he said, 'I'd like a word with you.'

I stopped; he was looking over my shoulder.

'Flanders . . .' he began.

'Listen,' I said. 'Listen carefully, because I'll deny every word I say when you report me for insubordination, and, more, I'll tell the C.O. that, ever since you came to Sinji, you've gone out of your way to hound me. And Wakerly—I'll tell how you victimised him because of Budmouth and Caroline Driffield, how you got him down so he didn't care what happened any more. You can let that lie on what passes with you for a conscience; he was ten times the man you are. And Glapthorn . . . even *him* . . . why did he have to have his nose pushed in the mud?'

The words came tumbling out and I took a step closer to him.

'Well, they've tumbled to you at last. There isn't a chap on the Station that doesn't loathe you. And Caroline—now that she knows—as she must—what you really are—poor kid. . . .' In the distance I saw someone approaching from the billets: it was time to go.

Turton had gone deathly pale. For the first time I saw that he was holding a cablegram. Then I turned and left him.

'Flanders,' he called after me, 'Flanders, there's something I want to tell you. . . .'

I didn't turn but went ploughing on through the dust and heat.

He didn't report me. He knew that he'd had it. He knew that I meant what I'd said, that I'd bring him down with me.

I hoped I'd never set eyes on him again.

Twenty-Four

Things were happening quickly now. Between the game against the Station and the end of my time at Sinji there were but a few days. I remember clearly when the last jag began—one afternoon when I returned from work to the billet.

'That opera singer,' Pouncey was saying . . . 'she was *massive*. When she lay on me it was like being in the belly of a whale. One night I thought I was going to die from lack of air. I hammered at her sides and yelled, "Let me out, let me out!" After that I always stayed on top.'

'Liar!' sniggered Pinkney.

'It's God's truth,' Pouncey said. 'Nearly every night after the show, Traviata, Trovatore, Aida, Carmen—you name it, she sang it—we went to posh parties. All the Impresarios and Aristocracy and Stars of Shows! Noilly Prat flowed like bathwater (you do have a bath in your tenement, Pinkney?). Your chick had to be wearing mink or ermine or back the bouncers threw you. They brought round caviare heaped on damned big dishes. You daren't put your goblet down or someone sloshed it full of Napoleon brandy '25.'

'Never mind about the party,' [Pinkney]. 'What happened after?'

'About two or three in the morning we'd go back to *her* suite. She'd knock up the maid ("What else are the slaves for but to be inconvenienced, darling?" she used to say) and make her cook us an absolutely mountainous breakfast. (She used to insist I ate a heap of eggs to tone me up.) Then we'd

165

go to bed; it was double size, silk sheets, mirrors everywhere, the ceiling was one big looking-glass, and we'd pig it until lunch came up. . . .'

'You had it in bed with her?'

'Where else?'

'And after you'd finished it?'

'Then a fag—scented Egyptians—for me. She used to light and hold it for me. . . .'

'And then . . .?'

And then a maintenance sergeant came in.

'Good news for you, Pouncey,' he said. 'You've been honoured by the Section and unanimously elected to do an air test with that renowned pilot, F/O Gawkrodger-Jones.'

In the RAF there was a fiendishly clever routine of testing flights after a major inspection. The tradesmen responsible for the maintenance went for a compulsory flip with the crew—electrician, rigger, fitter, instrument basher, radio mechanic and so on—one from each kind, like the Ark—just to see if adjustments were still needed. Or so they said. Well, that was part of the reason; you have to concede that. But look at it another way. What rigger wanted to fly if he thought there was a chance a wing he'd signed as airworthy might drop off? And if a fitter signed that his engines were hundred per cent efficient, what he really meant was that he personally felt safe behind them at four thousand feet. It was a solemn antidote for shoddy work!

Evidently, there was to be one of these exercises of daring next day.

'Desperate Dan,' everybody chanted, 'Desperate Dan,'
'The Olde Original Miracle Man,
All that keeps him in the air
Is his agèd grandma's bedside prayer.'

'Leave us your U.K. address,' someone yelled, 'and I'll write all your boy friends and tell them though you lived like a woman, you died like a man.' And someone asked, 'Who will Pinkney marry when he's a widower?'

Usually Pouncey could cope very well with this stuff but not this time: he was frightened. There was a strong element of truth in the twitting and he knew it. So he didn't answer, went on looking a bit green and pretended to write a letter.

An aircrew sergeant came in just then. I didn't know him but some of the others did.

'There he is, Sarge,' they shouted. 'That green man. Which wing has he to ride on?'

'Hey, Pouncey, Dan's sent it in writing that he won't bounce more than five times coming in.'

'Sixth time, he'll just keep on diving,' someone added.

But the sergeant came to me and said that B's navigator would like me to go up next day and work the camera because Group H.Q. had asked them to do a mosaic of the swamps north of town for the Governor's office; they'd been detailed to carry on with this when they'd finished the air-test. It really was nothing to do with me. My job was to service cameras and process films and, in this case, to develop prints and lay the mosaic. Operation of the camera was a navigator's job as well he knew. He'd been trained for it, even though he probably hated working a T.35 Control for fear of making a mess of the job and getting a rocket from the C.O.

The sergeant looked a bit lame when he asked me. He knew what the lads thought about flying with Dan and, what is more, knew *he* wouldn't have gone sailing with him in a lifeboat on a village duckpond. But I thought, What the heck! It'll get around fast if I refuse. He's not likely to want me again. So I said I'd go unless a lot of extra work came in.

I didn't tell anyone what he'd wanted and went on writing to my mother. But Pouncey must have heard be-

167

cause, when I glanced up, he was staring at me. I pretended not to notice: he gave me the creeps and, as I've said before, we ignored each other. Now I guessed he knew that I was in the same boat as himself and that had established something. Well, I thought, I don't fancy dicing with Dan any more than you do, Pouncey, but I'm hanged if I'm going to show *you* that.

Then, about two or three in the morning, I woke up. There was the usual groaning and gasping but there was something different too. I couldn't believe it at first but it was there all right: Pouncey was jabbering very softly to himself and, now and then, sobbing. It was revolting.

Twenty-Five

I turned up at about ten, humping an F.24 with a five-inch
lens (we used an eight-inch for normal jobs) and sat dangling
my legs over the planks of the jetty idly looking down at
the millions of tiny crabs burrowing and emerging from
the mud. An M.B.C. dinghy man was lolling in his boat
humming Nellie Dean. After about five minutes, B's crew,
looking grim and surly, arrived in a light van. But it shook
me more than somewhat when I saw Turton was with them;
evidently he was coming for a flip. He was laughing a lot
to cover his nerves I expect, but no-one took much notice
of him and it occurred to me that, as with Glapthorn, when
the heat was on from up top, no-one wanted a blast by staying too close to the victim.

Ha, I thought, so you're trying to pull yourself back
from where the new C.O. kicked you, letting the Mess see
that you're not just a commissioned clerk. Well, I bet you
don't know as much as the rest of us about a dice with Dan:
there's a lot easier way of getting some flying-time in.

Desperate Dan himself, as usual, was spraying orders in
all directions (often cancelling themselves out). He didn't
greet me: I was part of the luggage.

The rest of the servicing bods were already aboard making a last check to ensure their safe return. Besides Pouncey,
there was a flight mech, a radio mech and an electrician.
Pouncey himself looked listless and the other three jumpy.
They pushed all five of us amidships and I sat with the
F.24, its spare magazine between my legs. Turton began to
show a fussy interest in the navigator, but Desperate made

no exceptions in his bossiness and told him to go amidships too. We all sat pretty close together, but he looked forwards and I looked at the blisters towards the tail. Everyone began to put on Mae Wests with greatest care except us trades-men: there weren't any for us. Desperate Dan inspired the greatest air-safety-precautions in any crew in the air forces of the entire world I should imagine. You always had the idea that the whole bunch of them had their eyes on the nearest exit at take-off and landing. If anything goes wrong, I thought, won't there be a stampede!

B's engines began to roar as she warmed up. Then she taxied to the starting line and began her run-up. The water rumbled underfoot, followed by that ghastly scraping din under her keel, like a rake being dragged across a corru-gated tin roof. Then clouds of spray drenched the port-holes and mercifully shut out the sight of the mangroves racing past. The engines were making one massive, strangled roar as though they'd blow up and, as always, I wondered why anyone risked his neck on the word of fit-ters and the Catalina Aircraft Corporation. Then she lifted abruptly, as though Dan had pulled her into the air by the scruff of the neck and, after that, the engines didn't sound so hard pushed. The wings swayed and we began to tip side-ways so that I could see an African staring up from his hovel and, then, astonishingly, Trader's sandbar and his two concubines sunning themselves, then a jumble of chan-nels and, beyond, the ocean's tide-lines wrinkled along the glittering beaches. And, all this time, we were leaning against the air in a massive turn.

The air-test took about ten minutes and everything was O.K., because I saw the flight-engineer give thumbs-up and the flight-mech, looking relieved, came back amidships and shouted something at Pouncey who relaxed. It must have shaken them when they discovered B was staying up for another half-hour whilst the mosaic was being done.

A W/op must have got the order on his intercom because he told me to lay the camera. So I retreated nervously to the tunnel door, unbarred it and crawled inside, hearing him shoot the bolt fastening me in. I clipped on the safety belt which hung from a steel cable and sceptically wondered if it would hold me if I fell out. And, if I did, what would it be like dangling six feet below B and a couple of thousand feet above the ocean. And if anyone would notice that I'd gone. All quite ridiculous of course, but that's the way you thought when they shut you in the tunnel.

I'd lie if I say that I enjoyed flying. I always was relieved to be back at Height Nought. On top of that, in a Catalina's tail, you couldn't stand or even sit. All you could do was kneel—bent slightly forwards off balance, like a constipated heathen supplicating his god. It was a queer business.

However, I took a deep breath, averted my eyes and unlocked the camera hatch, pushed it up and away from me and pretended not to see the sea through the horrifying gap below. [If you let your imagination run, you could see yourself shrinking small enough to be sucked through the camera frame even when I'd dropped it into position.] Wind came rushing up, and it was cold all of a sudden.

Someone began to shake my shoulder and I gingerly turned my head; the Second Pilot's face was so close that I couldn't focus it. He pushed a helmet and headphones at me and I put them on and listened. It was funny really, when he was so close to me.

'Is the camera ready?'

'Yes, sir.'

'Flanders reports camera ready, Skipper.'

'This is the Captain, Flanders. Is the camera at readiness?'

(This was typical of everything that went on. Bags of bull plastering up the whacking big cracks in Dan's Fred Karno outfit.)

'Yes, sir. Will you please test it.'

'Switching on camera—now.'

'It's working . . . operating, sir.'

'I should hope so.'

'I'll fit the magazine, sir.'

The Navigator broke into the crackle. 'Set five degrees starboard drift.'

'Yes, sir. Five degrees starboard drift.'

So I set it and was settling back when there was this hand twisting my shoulder again. It was the Second Pilot who'd been listening-in to all this palaver and now glared furiously at me and broke into the circuit to tell me to take my finger out and remember that the aircraft and the camera were travelling in different directions for the purposes of a mosiac and that I'd set five degrees *port* drift. I changed this and heard myself being locked in again. I heard him reporting my stupidity to Desperate Dan who immediately began an argument with the Navigator, who shut him up by telling him we were about to begin a run and to start the camera. The T.35 began to tick off the intervals, the red light flashed, then the green, then the disc shot round and the gearbox crashed the first cycle home.

And then, as usual, the heaving and bumping around in the tunnel made me sick and, as a matter of fact, it was whilst I was vomiting past the lens down the hole that I heard the panic signal from Operations in Sinji.

It was Control telling Desperate that a Liberator from Sierra Leone, at the limit of its patrol, had reported a very strong possible sighting of a surfaced U-boat coming north into our area. Control was ordering B to proceed immediately to the given position.

I could feel the Cat wheeling but, in the flap, no-one told me to switch off the camera so, for about fifteen minutes, the red and green clicked merrily whilst I photographed a few hundred thousand acres of Mid-Atlantic. Then they must have remembered, because the hatch was released and a sergeant/air-gunner beckoned me out, pulled off my helmet and yelled in my ear that I was to shut up shop and come on out of it.

'And don't worry,' he yelled. 'Even if it was a Jerry (which I doubt) Dan won't find it. He couldn't find the *Queen Mary*.' He'd taken off his own helmet but, as I stumbled past him, he picked it up and listened with one ear, raised his eyes to the roof and passed it to me.

Desperate and the Second Pilot (an Australian) and the Navigator were having a real three-way set-to. The Navigator was insisting that Dan wasn't taking the correct routine to give him adequate time to work out the correct drift (they used to drop a smoke float) and the Second Pilot was protesting that they hadn't enough fuel for a search so far out. (He kept repeating, 'In my *considered* opinion you will be putting this aircraft in jeopardy.') But I reckon Dan could smell a gong (Immediate Award) and wasn't going to have it snatched away by technicalities. All the same, I remember thinking he'd make a pretty poor captain of a cricket club if he let his side argue the toss like that with him.

Turton had gone to the Navigator's table and put on an expression of intelligent interest. What went on in his head I don't even begin to know. Pouncey, looking pale, had laid down and closed his eyes. The flight-mech, radio-mech and the electrician looked wooden and it was plain wouldn't come alive again until they told the tale amid shrieks of laughter in their billets. I really can't remember how I felt, but I do recall making a mental note *never* to fly again with this shower.

I moved back to my appointed dark hole amidships and sat on a bunk, as usual wondering which would be the best exit to take—front or back—if the worst came to the worst. Then I saw Desperate look over his shoulder, see Turton, and wave angrily at him to get back with us. He flushed and sat opposite me, our knees almost touching. I looked steadfastly backwards at the gunners in their blisters and decided they'd got a really bad attack of the screamers (they were a ghastly lot), but I knew that he was looking at me.

I suppose he must have realised at long last that he and I meant more to each other than anyone else on B—we'd touched each other's lives through Glapthorn, that last fantastic game of cricket and, further back still, there were Wakerly, Budmouth and Caroline to connect us. Many a time since I've wondered if, all at once and for the first time in his life, he knew that class and rank don't mean a thing when the cards are down. I felt he wanted to speak to me, to tell me something I ought to know. If he had the screamers, at least he didn't show it like Pouncey. He was like I'd seen him when he wore his gas-cape, when he was in the ranks at Budmouth, that time in the rain when the rest of us daren't. I realised with a start that I'd been looking at him, examining his faint smile and his sharp nose lifted as though he was smelling what the form was.

I felt a hand on my arm; it was Pouncey. 'What's going to happen, Flanders?'

I shook my head. And moved my arm.

'I'm scared,' he said. 'I hope to God I get out of this. I wish I'd refused to fly with him; I'd sooner have a court-martial than this. I don't think they know what they're doing. That Dan's crazy. . . .'

He gabbled on. If Turton heard him, he didn't show it and I looked as wooden as I could. I suppose it would have helped him if I'd said what he wanted me to—that I wasn't too happy either. But, with Pouncey, that wasn't safe. He couldn't be trusted. When he'd got himself safe back to the billet, he'd make up some lying tale. ('Flanders looked distinctly green, darlings: one big twitch from arse to heel!')

As a matter of fact, whenever I flew, I tried to make myself go wooden. Wakerly used to say there was only one way to tolerate flying—to decide irrationally to have an absolute and quite unjustified confidence in the pilot. But that wasn't for me. I felt no more confidence in any pilot than I did in any captain of any cricket side, except myself. That was my nature—then. So I sat woodenly waiting for Desperate to bitch it up and, when he did, to stir, as best I could, for myself.

Frankly, I don't think he (D.D.) had any plan at all in his crazy head and I just hoped to God that, if there *was* a U-boat, its captain had seen the Stirling and had had the sense to submerge. But I consoled myself thinking that the Navigator would never find the spot anyway.

But he did.

Even before one of the gunners beckoned me to the blister I knew it: it was as if the temperature had shot up twenty degrees at a flick of a switch. And there it was, the U-boat, going gently along like a pleasure-boat on a flat sea. It was like a page in a picture-book. I thought, This isn't like the War you read about in the *Mirror*; it's all too easy.

Anyway, he must have seen us almost as soon as we saw him because he changed course at right angles to us. There were a couple of men in his conning tower and that, probably, was the reason why he made no attempt to dive. You could see the point of that: submerging over-late was worse than staying on top. There, at least, you could face up to your attacker, whereas if you couldn't drop deeper than a couple of hundred feet, you'd just be depth charged to the surface in bits.

Desperate was making a clumsy manoeuvre to come in with the sun as they'd taught him at flying-school, and evidently he was combining this with a closer look at his victim. But, being him, he went *too* close. It was the Jerry gunner on his tower who spoiled things. By all the rules that Dan had learnt, this gunner should have waited until

175

we began our run in before defending himself. But this stalwart knew that desperate occasions need desperate action. (Anywhere else, I'd have given him a clap!) So he let fly as we were passing broadside. The odds were all against him because, when his trial burst had told him just what adjustment his gun needed, we should have changed direction and height.

The trouble was that he pulled it off first time. His first and only burst, one incredible fluke, went through B's hull like a buzz-saw. Naturally, amidships, I didn't see what *did* happen, except that there was a brilliant flash in my face, then I saw daylight through a jagged gash in the metal and felt wet on the palm of my hand. And, whilst I was still looking with astonishment at the blood oozing from under my cuff, I was thrown to my knees and then flat on my face with something heavy across my back. I tried to struggle up but couldn't because of the pull as B dived. Odd as it may seem, I remember thinking how powerful centrifugal force was: it glued me to the floor.

I knew we were going to hit the sea but it was all happening too fast to be scared. I scrambled to my feet as B levelled out, turning to slip from whatever was on my back. It turned out that this was Pouncey. Well I say it was Pouncey, but I only *guessed* it was, because he'd got it in the face and, as he slipped past me, all I saw was that his face wasn't there, just a crimson mask. But it could only have been him because the other three and one gunner had been thrown back against the tunnel hatch and the other gunner was on his knees, his hands on his throat and blood pumping through his fingers. He just stared solemnly at me.

I turned round. Somebody, it could have been Turton or the Navigator, was picking himself up by the table. The Second Pilot (who was strapped in) was dragging at the controls. It must have been him who had got us out of the dive. I couldn't see round the corner, but I expect Desperate

Dan must have bought it. So I turned again and began to struggle back to the blisters. That was when he brought her down on the sea. It was like slashing across eight acres of emery paper—a plain miracle her bottom wasn't ripped out. Then she bounced up and hit again like a hare shot at full gallop. By this time I was down again with what was left of Pouncey, and the next thing I knew was salt water swilling into my mouth and somebody trampling over me. He even put his big feet on my head. Once again I got up. B had keeled over on her side, water pouring in through the submerged blister, whilst the other was like a sky-light, and the Navigator was standing on the gunner's seat, clawing at a ledge with one hand and pushing at the perspex dome with the other. And it opened. Then he switched both hands to the window-sill (as you might say) and pushed blindly through to the air.

God, I thought, I'll never get out now. By the time he's through I'll be trapped. I distinctly remember that. I stumbled up behind him. One of his arms was dripping blood and, as he tried to drag himself out, he made gasps and whines, noises like an animal. I began to push him. Then I felt him crumple like a bit of wet card and he slipped back through my arms like a sack of grain.

I took his place and pushed myself head first into the sea and lurched for a dinghy that had automatically inflated and was flopping about beside B. What happened to the Navigator I don't know. He must have been dying as he fell back. Anyway, it was out of the question for me to have helped him. How could I have got him out in that state? It isn't a liner I'm talking about. Just an open blister, a sky-light, in a sinking aircraft.

Getting myself into the dinghy was a nightmare. It bucked and crumpled and twisted like a live thing. But, eventually, I got my head and shoulders over the side and wriggled till I was more in than out and then lay with my head on the bottom, panting and gasping and moaning, throwing up salt water and hearing the sea rasping at the rubber skin. Thinking back, I reckon I was chiefly afraid I'd be a fool and go back after that Navigator.

And, when I pulled myself in and sat up, I saw that B had gone. There was nothing to show where she'd floated but my cap, sodden and ready to sink.

Then I saw Turton: just his head hanging back, eyes closed, his chin up in the air, a Mae West holding up his chest, rising and falling in the swell. The rest of him must have been hanging in a curve. He must have been thrown clear through the forward perspex and hit something as he came. He was no more than a couple of yards away. Would I have tried to pull him in? Ah, that's the question and I'll leave it at that.

The U-boat moved in very near. It was so close and I was so low in the water that it stood over me like a house-end. An officer and a couple of ratings looked down curiously at me.

'You left only?' he called.

A rating touched his arm and pointed at the Adjutant's head appearing and disappearing.

'Will not you pull him in? Is he drownded?'

He looked quizzically at me. Did he guess?

I nudged the dinghy over and went on my knees, got Turton under the arms and tugged at him. It was hell's own job, but, eventually, with a bit of help at the right time from the swell, I had him slopping over the side and propped him on the floor beside me, his head hanging back.

'Do you savvy where you are?' the officer called.

I shook my head.

'One hundred ten kilometre west of Konakri. You understand?'

I nodded.

'You come out from Sierra Leone?'

I didn't answer.

'Never mind, Johnny Bull, we know. We know all about you. Sorry. I cannot aid you.' He grinned suddenly. 'Maybe your pilot have time to say Mayday, Mayday, on radio before he prang. You see, we know all about RAF. You must take pot-luck. Have you refreshments?'

I held up an emergency pack. 'Nothing,' I shouted. 'Only this.'

'We will spare a little water,' he called, 'and a little grub.' And one of his men threw a couple of aluminium canisters where I could reach them.

'Well, I'm sorry for you, old chap. But it was you or us. Good luck!'

He left the turret and the men followed him. She disappeared below the surface as swiftly as a stone drops. One minute he was talking, the next there was only sea. . . .

804. 821. U-BOAT. ATTACK. 30.1.43. F/14"

Twenty-Six

Turton was only an arm's length from me, so close that our knees were touching. So I had to look at him. And heavens, what a mess he was! Hair plastered to the scalp, his uniform as tight as an extra skin! But, oddly, no sight of a wound. Yet, though I never worked out what he'd hit or what had hit him, he must have been damaged inside—badly—because he breathed like a man under water, in gurgles. And another thing—his eyes were open even though I was quite sure he couldn't see.

I felt that I ought to take off his mae-west but, frankly, I didn't like touching him. So, after looking at him for a while, I began to think about myself, what the form was, what sort of a chance I had, what would happen to me.

The sea was calm, just a gentle swell rising and falling, and the dinghy rose and gently fell with it. (But, all the same, I couldn't help reflecting that only a very thin skin of yellow rubber lay between me and sinking a mile deep.) The sun was hot and, though my thick fair hair was some help, it was a great relief to tie on Wakerly's crazy scarf like a turban.

The worst thing was the silence. In the end, I had to say something.

'Well, here we are,' I said, 'a small ad-hoc committee (as Slingsby would have said in twice as many words). In the Chair—the true and undoubted captain of A 697 Squadron C.C., Aircraftsman 2nd Class Flanders, T., and the self-styled captain, Flight-Lieutenant Turton, initials unknown but bound to be Something, Something, Something. Natur-

180

ally! Apologies? Yes, from the Secretary, Slingsby, detained crocheting a way to his young lady's heart. And Wood and Stone, poor Wood, poor Stone. Wickets-chalked-on-the-playground-wall cricketers! But gentlemen. Undoubtedly! "The people of the heathen bow down to wood and stone," don't they, Turton? They do—it's in a hymn in the Wesleyan Hymnal Foreign Missions Section. And Horn, T.—happily busying himself on the bosoms of his family. Lastly, Aircraftsman 1st Class W-Wakerly. P. N. V.—alas, detached elsewhere. . . .'

His pale eyes never left my face for a moment. But they had no intelligence in them. I might as well have talked to a beast in the foldyard.

'Minutes of the last meeting. "As far as circumstances permitted, the programme arranged was completed except in A/C Flanders' head. It was therefore agreed to disband the Club, pending unforeseen developments. . . ." Now, there's an interesting point. . . . Can we say that this is "an unforeseen development"—you and me in a blown-up boat, together at last, to play out time. But, surely, even Slingsby, Ossett prophet, can't have foreseen *this*?'

There was not a flicker on his face: he sat like a stupid, obedient child.

'Agenda? This could take the form of an enquiry. Yes, of course, an Enquiry. We both have considerable experience of enquiries. We *could* enquire why 697 Cricket Club didn't complete the programme in A/C Flanders' head. But we should have to dig deep. And there's the difficulty of calling witnesses—Fife, Glapthorn, Mr. Ridd, Wakerly . . . Caroline Driffield. I mean to say it began so much longer ago than Sinji, didn't it? You never knew what he wrote on his pub-map, did you? Wakerly, I mean—

> "A guardian angel tends The Vine—
> Sweetest of girls, dear Caroline."

Would that be considered evidence? But you can't answer the questions that ought to be asked. Why you had to have her? Why, if you really loved her, did you have to make her pregnant first? Were you afraid that, given a little longer, she might have seen through you to a man worth ten Turtons?'

(But, even so, I thought, Wakerly would still be dead. Losing Caroline didn't kill him, or even losing his grip. There were others who died when K crashed, men who wanted to live. . . .)

The sun's heat was intense, bewildering: it grew harder to keep my mind on things, to keep talking.

'And me . . .' I said. 'What about me? I loved her too. Even Wakerly never knew that. But that's not surprising. I'm only telling you because you're on your way out and can never repeat it. . . .'

I bent towards him. 'But I'm going to make it, Turton. Do you understand? I'm going to make it. I'm going back to Budmouth. I'm going back to Budmouth'—I shouted it. 'To her.'

Of course he didn't answer; he couldn't possibly have understood.

The sea sparkled in the sunlight. A bit of a swell had come up and we rode gently across low hills of water. I wanted to sleep but I knew that I must stay awake just in case anything turned up. I fell asleep.

When I woke the sea had flattened again and there was a great hush. It was dark, so dark that, until the moon rose, I couldn't even see Turton. And, when it did rise, it was one of the most beautiful nights I can remember; clouds had gathered to the south and lay like fields of snow in the moonlight. And Turton—still the same rasping gulps of breath, spasmodically, as if each intake of air was his last. He sagged more like a heap of clothes than a man.

There's one thing certain, I thought, you're going first.

And another is that I'm going to live. I'm not going to die here. I'm going back. I'm not giving in. It's my turn. Some day I'll tell her what really happened at Sinji. And . . . Wakerly, we'll remember and talk about him. But this one. . . .

That was when he heaved up as if shaken from a nightmare and shuddered and opened his eyes. I was pleased that he didn't know where he was or who he was with; there was too much between us. Battered dummy as he was, I still hated him for what he'd done to Wakerly and for what he'd done to me. Not so much the cricket but making me despise myself.

'You're going to die soon,' I said. 'And, if I thought there was even a thousand to one chance of you making it, I'd roll you out now.'

His expression never changed; his eyes like a dog's, trying to understand. And you might just as well have talked to a dog.

Whether I slept again that night I can't say. Soon afterwards, the clouds thickened and covered the sky. But for the hiss of water scraping the dinghy, we could as well have been in the middle of a field. An hour before dawn there was a tropical storm; lightning flickered around the horizon, wind blew in gusts like a blower switched on and off, haphazard. There were crackles of thunder, and rain swept across, leaving the dinghy's bottom swilling with water.

After the first hour in that dinghy, I can truthfully say that I never was really afraid. By nature, I'm the sort who watches for a change. Farming makes you that way. Things don't stay set for long—drought, waterlogged fields, bad harvests. You have to wait; there's always a break if you're ready for it. It's a matter of hanging on, sitting it out. Once you begin to believe a situation is unalterable, you might as well pack up. It was the same now. I agree that time was scarce. Down to hours in fact. But so long as the weather stayed clear, there was always a chance that one of our own aircraft would find us. I had great confidence in that navigator: he was the sort of binder who would—to his last gasp—insist on going through 'the correct procedure'. He didn't look the type who'd panic and I felt that, before B bought it, he must have made the W/op signal our position to Sinji or Somewhere.

It became light with a rush as, in those latitudes, it always did. For a few minutes there was an almost transparent film of cloud in the air, and then its skin was torn away and the sun glared down. The heat struck at once. Think of the hottest day you can remember: it was like that and still only daybreak.

I nibbled two or three of the biscuits, going round and round their rims to make them last longer. And a drink of the water, letting a teaspoonful at a time trickle down my throat. To tell you the truth, I didn't know what to do about Turton. His eyes were still open. I held out the canister to him, but he didn't take it; he didn't look at it even. I've wondered since if I shouldn't have wriggled across and tried to force some down his throat, but I couldn't make myself touch him. His right hand rested on a knee, so I put a biscuit on it. He stayed absolutely motionless: at mid-day the biscuit still balanced there, as he still stared stupidly over my shoulder.

I remember once reading how an American, as an experiment, took his stand at a busy New York corner and began to gaze at the sky. There was nothing there but, a half hour later, the street was filled by people staring up too. It was the same now. I knew that Turton couldn't see anything—even if there *was* anything—because he'd lost touch. But all the same, like an itch, I felt I had to look too. So I pretended to feel behind my back as though I was uncomfortable and gave myself an excuse to carefully turn sideways and then over on to my knees, facing backwards.

A ship was moving south at right angles to us, very distant, one mile or more, so far that it was almost a silhouette, but not too far that I couldn't tell from its superstructure that it was a medium-sized freighter. And since it wasn't in convoy, I supposed it was a neutral, a Portuguese going round the Cape to Mozambique or a Spaniard bound for Fernando Po.

I scrambled round [so rapidly that the dinghy flopped alarmingly] and stared at Turton. He wasn't looking at the boat now: he was looking at me. It was the first time we'd looked at one another since . . . I was going to say, since we'd been together on the dinghy . . . but it was the first time we'd ever really looked at one another. We'd seen each other but not *looked*, groped, as you might put it, into each other's mind, groped and wondered what we'd find.

There'd been only a shadow of a change. A brightening of the eyes, a slight lowering of the brow. But it meant that he'd been watching that freighter all right. And it must have passed quite close to us. And I knew that he read my thoughts, as I struggled to contain my anger. More than that—he was amused that I refused to make any connection with him, even in hate.

I unloosened Wakerly's scarf and, once again, carefully twisted round, pushed first one foot, then another to the extremity of the dinghy and very carefully straightened my knees. For some moments I struggled to balance. The freighter had already gone further away, and I panicked as I waved the scarf in long sweeps to its full extent and went on and on, changing arms as I tired. On and on mechanically, until the hull grew to a dot and then, despairingly, to a band of smoke trailing low on the horizon.

Then I sat down. Turton hadn't moved or made a sound. So I looked at him again. He looked back, straight into my eyes. Then his lips pursed, one corner of his mouth twisted slightly and, for an an instant, his eyes glinted. And it

185

struck me—You didn't want us to be seen. You don't care one way or the other. No, more than that—you don't want to survive. You've worked out that, either way, you've had it. You've thrown your hand in. Like Glapthorn. Like Wakerly. And you want to make sure I go out with you.

And then I twisted my eyes away, watching the rough skin of the ocean.

Twenty-Seven

Well, I blacked out soon after that. The heat was staggering. You couldn't get away from it. You had to take it. It was like a crazy rule of the I Zingari Club, I remember reading—

> 'New members will take their stand in the nets without bat or pads for a period to be decided upon by a committee member present and there remain whilst being bowled at by other members . . .'

When I came to, Turton was moving. He had begun vaguely to rub his scalp; the sun was hitting him hard and his thin ginger hair was no protection at all. He was muttering too: nothing you could understand. And he went on like this for some time, perhaps an hour.

Then his eyes glazed over.

I thought, if I get out of this, I'll have to tell her. Or she'll guess how it was, that I watched him being finished off by the sun. It will always be between us.

So I bent over, gradually eased myself to my knees and, not looking at him, bound the scarf in a rough turban round his head. Then I sat back.

'Wakerly's scarf,' I said. 'If anything's happening in your silly head, think over that one.'

God, it was hot. The sky might have been on fire. I didn't know where to put myself. I pushed my hands under my shirt; I tried to protect my legs by rubbing them with sea water. (But that made it worse.) And I was so confused, that

I began to imagine that the dinghy itself might well catch fire.

I must have been in a pretty bad way that afternoon. I knew I was rambling, but not so bad that I couldn't worry that Turton might understand me. I knew that I was repeating things other people had said. Till then, I'd never really known how much of me was an empty drum answering echoes. Things my mother used to say when I was a lad, Wakerly, Caroline, even Turton himself—a stream of nonsense dribbling out into the vast emptiness of heat as I reeled around Sinji, Budmouth, Blackfen, the poor old *Mungo Park*, Wintersghyll. . . .

In clearer spells, I thought how like a game of cricket this story of Turton and myself had been. Players had come and taken their stand or swung their arms and had gone. And the issue had wavered this way and that, but chiefly it had gone his way. But now the game, if you can call it that, was near its end. He had lost: that much was certain. But had I won?

I lost something at Sinji, and its last shred went that afternoon. Those last hours with Turton destroyed what I thought I was. We all lost. One after the other. All along the way from The Vine to this. Me last of all—because, until then, I still believed every game must have a winner.

As evening came on—though in those latitudes, evening is not as we know it—I became more or less normal and drank some water and, once more, nibbled three biscuits. I bent over to Turton but, again, he didn't reach for the canister. I still didn't know what to do about him. Plainly, he'd been very seriously damaged when he'd been thrown from B. But what went on in his head? Sometimes, I thought he knew what the form was but didn't care, and sometimes I thought he was only semi-conscious and didn't even know where he was or who he was with. But he was there and, so long as he was, I made myself do something for him. I knew, now, that I didn't want to be left alone. So I eased myself to my knees again and pushed the canister at his face, the nozzle to his lips. But he didn't open them. I felt his teeth against the metal.

'Drink,' I said. 'You've got to drink or you'll die.' He was looking dead at me, at first with no expression in his eyes. Then I thought I caught a puzzled look. Perhaps I didn't. It was no use: he wouldn't take it, and I leaned back again.

'I don't think you even *want* to live,' I yelled. 'You've given up. You can't take it. . . .'

There I stopped myself: that way lay madness.

The second night came suddenly. The dinghy flapped gently as flurries of breeze caught and twisted it. Except for gurgles from air trapped between the rubber skin and the sea, it was as still as the grave.

It was a long night. When people ask me what you think of in a mess like that, I have to admit that, for most of the time, your mind is a blank; you don't care. I reckoned that, though I'd enough water and biscuits to keep me going for maybe a week, the sun would finish me within two more days: I'd either be dead or crazy. But I'd already decided from watching Turton that the end wasn't going to be all that bad, because I wouldn't know what was going on.

It won't be so bad, I kept thinking, if my brain dies before my body: I don't want to keep on thinking. I've had enough.

What is it all about? Life, I mean. What makes us tick? Love, hate, just sheer doggedness? Not hate. It can only corrode, eat at your spirit, destroy what it feeds on. If I'd had the blind faith of my grandad or my mother—as he dredged into his Bible, as she knelt on the cold lino in the cold bedroom talking confidently into the blackness! But for me there was Nothing. Just me, what I was, what they'd

189

made me, what I'd let myself become. There I was—groping, without purpose, alone.

The sea made no sound. There were only the stars, larger than over The Vale: the sky was white with them. They glittered and burned, as they wheeled in the air. And it had been like this for a million years and would be for a million years: men creeping out from the blackness and sinking back into the blackness, touching a hand, exchanging a glance. Unknown even to themselves. And then forgotten.

It was about then that Turton began to moan: it was the first sound he'd made. Then he sat upright. (Till then he'd slumped back.) In the half-light of the stars I could see that he was staring at me and opening his mouth trying to speak. And he was moving his hands. He was pushing one hand out, inch by inch, till the fingers reached my wrist and fastened on it.

And that's how we stayed all night.

Sometimes I dozed but, whenever I awoke, he still held me. When it happened I don't know, but when dawn came, he was dead.

I unloosed his fingers and sat looking at him. Well, I thought, that's finished. Wakerly, Glapthorn, you. . . . And me on my last legs. As I unwrapped Wakerly's scarf and tied it round my own head again, I decided that it would be better if he went over the side straight away whilst I still had enough strength to do it. Then I thought he might have something useful in his pockets, perhaps a knife or even something to read.

It's odd that, alive, even as little alive as he'd been, I couldn't bring myself to touch him. But dead—it was easy. As I'd hoped, in his pockets I found a knife, but nothing else worth keeping. So I fished into his breast pocket which was buttoned. There was a letter postmarked two months before and it was from Caroline. I remember wondering why he'd not kept something more recent. It began,

190

'Darling, I won't write much because they tell me I mustn't until I'm quite well again. But before I go to sleep I must have a little talk to you. To tell you again how much I love and miss you. So terribly. More than ever. Write to me often and often and often. . . .'

I couldn't bring myself to read more. So she'd really loved him! For her, he'd not been the Turton we'd known! I'd never looked at it like that—that she might have seen him as no-one else did. I looked at him, twisted and suddenly shrunk and remembered him lying on the bed beside her, satisfied, smiling at the ceiling.

Well, I thought. In time, she will forget. And, in time, my turn will come. It's a matter of sitting it out.

Perhaps, I thought, All that has happened was meant to be—from the beginning. You see I felt certain now, absolutely certain that I was going to survive. Don't ask how or why—I felt it, suddenly—a lightening of my spirit.

Then I took hold of Turton's ankles and lifted his legs so that they hung above the water and I eased the rest of him over so that he didn't capsize the dinghy. And then, it only needed a nudge.

He slipped quietly in, feet first, no splash, no fuss, scarcely a stir in the water. All but his right arm: it was caught in the drogue line. As I freed it I saw some paper trapped in his hand and, as he slipped away, I forced it from his fingers.

I knew then that at some time—maybe at night, maybe when I was delirious—he had taken it from his pocket, perhaps even tried to read it.

It was as if he wanted me to have it. Before he sank, leaving me alone.

It was folded many times and, all at once, I knew it was that same piece of paper he had been reading on the gravel road the afternoon when he'd tried to speak to me, when I'd said the bitter things I did.

BE BRAVE CAROLINE PASSED AWAY PEACEFULLY THIS MORNING SHE WAS CONSCIOUS TO END HER LAST WORDS WERE DO NOT TELL NIGEL I AM SO ILL HE WOULD WORRY OUT THERE LETTER FOLLOWING GOD BLESS YOU MOTHER.

I read it again, then let it fall into the sea. It floated awhile, grew sodden and sank too.

Plan! There *was* no plan. You could organize the little things and kid yourself there was some system, but the big thing, Life itself, was a sprawling, shapeless, disgusting mess. It had about as much plan as a sow's litter.

I remember shivering in the baffling heat. Then sobbing on and on until darkness fell, bringing the rain.

Kettering 1967

THE QUINCE TREE PRESS was established by J.L. Carr as the publishing house for a series of 'Pocket Books' : small selections from the great poets (but exclusively those out of copyright); idiosyncratic Dictionaries, small Histories & volumes of Fabled Saying. Later a series of Wood Engravers, contemporary or near contemporary was added. The hand-drawn, poster-sized historical County Maps completed the early productions which together funded the self-employment which, in part, enabled the novels to be written.

The first six novels were initially published by conventional publishing houses, but as they went out of print the rights were reacquired and QTP editions produced. The last two novels 'H&F' and 'Hetty' were produced entirely in-house. An author's desire to be independent of the frustrations and irritations of the conventional publishing world was probably the incentive, but it developed to a positive pleasure in the design and production of a volume complementary to the text – there is a degree of unconventionality about all the productions.

The Novels, Pocket Books and Maps continue to be published by us and are available directly from us or through good booksellers.

THE QUINCE TREE PRESS
www.quincetreepress.co.uk

James Lloyd Carr attended the village school at Carlton Miniott in the North Riding and Castleford Secondary School; he taught for 37 years, finally as Headmaster of Highfields Primary in Kettering, Northamptonshire. He died in 1994.

A Month in the Country

A poignant tale of missed moments, love and discovery; set at the close of the Great War and enacted amongst a Yorkshire village community beneath the slowly unveiled mystery in the mediaeval wall-paintings of the church.

"During any prolonged activity one tends to forget original intentions. But I believe that, when making a start on *A Month in the Country*, my idea was to write an easy-going story, a rural idyll along the lines of Thomas Hardy's *Under the Greenwood Tree*. And, to establish the right tone of voice to tell such a story, I wanted its narrator to look back regretfully across forty or fifty years but, recalling a time irrecoverably lost, still feel a tug at the heart. And I wanted it to ring true. So I set its background up in the North Riding, on the Vale of Mowbray, where my folks had lived for many generations and where, in the plough-horse and candle-to-bed age, I grew up in a household like that of the Ellerbeck family.

Novel-writing can be a cold-blooded business. One uses whatever happens to be lying around in memory, and employs it to suit one's ends. The visit to the dying girl, a first sermon, the Sunday-school treat, a day in a harvest field and much more happened between the Pennine Moors and the Yorkshire Wolds. But the church in the fields is in Northamptonshire, its churchyard in Norfolk, its vicarage London. All's grist that comes to the mill.

Then, again, during the months whilst one is writing about the past, a story is coloured by the what presently is happening to its writer. So, imperceptibly, the tone of voice changes, original intentions slip away. And I found myself looking through another window at a darker landscape inhabited by neither the present nor the past."   J.L.Carr

"A profoundly affecting tale"   Auberon Waugh, *Evening Standard*

"It is short, it is odd, it is memorable, it is admirable"   Marghanita Laski

"... a book I have always loved. It was published first in 1980 and I liked it then, and now I like it even more. Some books work beautifully when one is young and also work well, but differently, when one is less young. This is one. It is a love story as all the best books are."   Michael Holroyd, *Sunday Telegraph*

ISBN 0-900847-92-1

 Winner of the Guardian Fiction Prize
Shortlisted for the Booker Prize
Filmed for Euston Films

How Steeple Sinderby Won the FA Cup

The title really is what this book is about, a fantastical ambition, but most importantly a mix of diverse characters who achieve it.

"Book-writing can be a tedious job needing some incentive to keep one at it. The impulse here was 'can this unbelievable feat be made to sound like the truth even though it didn't happen?' So I stacked the cards - a foreigner with remarkable theories, two young men with good reasons for having quit top-class football, a Chairman of napoleonic ability.

Then I dredged up memories of 1930 when I was an unqualified teacher, 18 years old and playing that single season for South Milford White Rose when we won a final which never ended. (Pitch invasion and furious fights are not new things.) I learnt much of rural life during that long-gone autumn, winter and early spring …

But is this story believable ? Ah, it all depends upon whether you <u>want</u> to believe it."

J.L. Carr, 1992

"He delivers with a kind of deceptive gaiety some murderous blows at the fatheads who populate professional football"   Benny Green

"It simply is the best football-based work of fiction"   David Taylor,
The London Magazine

❚ ISBN 0-900847-94-8   ISBN 0-900847-93-X ❚

Harpole and Foxberrow General Publishers

Books concern printers, publishers, sales reps, booksellers, proof-readers, professors, illustrators, indexers, critics, text editors, literary editors, librarians, book-reviewers and bookbinders and book-keepers, translators, typographers, Oxfam fund raisers, whole university departments of soothsayers, manufacturers of thread and glue, auctioneers, lumberjacks, starving mice, wolves howling at the doors of authors of first-novels, the Post Office's book-bashing machine minder, religious bonfire fuel suppliers and libel lawyers. And that this army is billeted upon one man or one woman gnawing a pen is neither here nor there.

So, by and large, this is what <u>this</u> book is about. It tries to answer Mrs Widmerpool's sister's alarming enquiry at George Harpole's trial, 'What <u>are</u> books ? Where do they come from ?'

Her 'Where do they go to ?' is unanswerable … except, quite often - to the head."

J.L. Carr

" It is as accomplished, as entertaining and as funny as anything its author has done."
D. J. Taylor, novelist, *The Spectator*

A DAY IN SUMMER

Hidden lives are exposed, secret memories unearthed in this wry, vivid novel, which moves like a thriller to its startling climax.

A Day in Summer that is the annual 'Feast' at Great Minden; a day of predictable delights and celebrations for the locals, and for many it may be so. But then the early train brings Peplow, intent on avenging his young son's death, killed by a feckless fairground lorry-driver.

The newcomer and the residents each have their own agenda, their own choices to make, their own pasts to deal with. Ruskin is an embittered ex-RAF pilot, confined to his wheelchair and the first floor flat with its view across the fair, living vicariously through the daily round of his neighbours. Whilst Croser, a libidinous young teacher must make a hapless choice between nubile but dull hairdresser Effie, or eloping with the Rector's exotic, restless wife Georgie.

As the characters and the sub-plots entwine, what is, at base, a thriller and tale of revenge becomes more of a black comedy. Departing on the evening train, Peplow is not the only one to consider the days events and to ponder its unexpected conclusions.

"His novel depends not on story and suspense but on the delightful, ironic and professional writing. My only fear is that he has come late to novel writing and used up too much observation and experience in his first book."
Thomas Hinde, *The Spectator*

"By mingling knockabout comedy and high seriousness Carr achieves a rare honesty, a kind of soured sweetness found in the work of no other contemporary writer."
D.J.Taylor, foreword to the Hogarth edition, 1986

Filmed by Yorkshire Television, with screenplay by Alan Plater, in 1988.

ISBN 1-904016-07-3

THE HARPOLE REPORT

The idea was to write a sort of text book for teachers and to tell parents more about what goes on in primary schools. And there is just about everything here - free meals, hymn-singing, caretakers, the New Maths, school visits, log-books, etc. etc. But Emma Foxberrow got out of hand and perhaps not so many readers take it seriously as about education. But some do and it has been said that all teachers whilst training should read it ....Any way it was all I wanted to say about a job I did for 9 years before the war and for 21 years after it.   J.L.Carr 1982

George Harpole is in his first term as Acting Head of Tampling St Nicholas Primary School and determined to climb the career ladder; the way ahead seems clear to teaching success. Little does he imagine that he'll be hampered by his honesty, fair mindedness, and a genuine liking for the children in his care (and then there are his fellow teachers to consider). They all contribute to his downfall, or at least to the point where iron enters his soul....

"The funniest and perhaps the truest story about running a school that I have ever read."   Frank Muir

"No aspect of state primary education is sacred to the author. While we laugh at it, however, we might keep in mind some of the recently published research findings on education and social class. The author means us to."
Times Literary Review

"Harpole remains quite the best book on the English School System. Brilliantly observed by a battle scarred veteran of the front line !"
Kenneth Baker, *Secretary of State for Education*

ISBN 1-904016-06-5

THE BATTLE OF POLLOCKS CROSSING

The story is told by an Englishman who, fifty years earlier, had taught for a single year in drought ravaged Dakota. Like many an English lad, George Gidner had a deep infatuation with the Wild West. When at twenty-five the chance came to spend a year teaching High School in the middle of South Dakota he grabbed it. So began his life as a foreigner, historian of the true heroes of the frontier, and a lifelong *affaire* with the Dakota plains.

Though he upset the establishment and lost his job, George had his fair share of admirers, from teenager Becky, to his landlord, Henry Farewell, manager of the Settler's Bank and hero of the Battle. The battle at the crossing is the denouement, collecting together the many threads of this tale of pioneering spirit; underlying all, however, is a warning that, although we technically share a language, the Americans may be disturbingly different.

"In 1938 it took me seven days to reach the prairie town where I had contracted to teach in its high school for a twelvemonth. An eight year drought had not ended, there had been bank-crashes: deserted quarter-sections could be bought merely by paying off back taxes. I found folk unfailingly friendly, helpful and kind, yet, at the year's end the United States still seemed to me a very foreign land. Plainly there was something about the Americas which I had failed to fathom and, in this story, I have tried to hint at this unease.

Yet, at the same time, I must remind those of my countrymen who read this novel that it was written during the 1980s, those years when we loitered warily and dangerously between East and West, two areas possessing immense power of destruction."   J.L. Carr, 1993

"It reconstructs a distant and dust-shrouded world, then sets it echoing with an outburst of violence."   Peter Kemp, *Sunday Times*

"This novel is hard to classify. To say it is funny and sad and exciting is inadequate. Comedy and seriousness are woven together so skilfully that the effect is both unexpected and satisfyingly natural. J.L. Carr is a wholly original writer and he has written a lovely book quite unlike any other."
Nina Bawden

ISBN 0-900847-96-4

Short-listed for the Booker Prize 1986

An eighteen year-old Sixth Form girl tells what happened to her when she left her Fenland home determined never to return.

Hetty is a spirited, intellectual girl, sustained by English literature in her struggles against a brutish home life (bullying fox-terrier of a father, timid and downtrodden mother, and nasty little brother eager for her downfall to spare his own hide). Apart from school friends her favoured companions are Keats and Browning.

When she discovers that she was in fact adopted, Hetty runs away from home, in search of her real parents. She finds shelter in Rose Gilpin-Jones' boarding house in Birmingham, where there are eccentric lodgers (one of whom, Emma Foxberrow, we have met in earlier novels) with telling tales, and experiences the wider world of ethics, music hall and mass demonstrations. After many tribulations eventually she finds her root-stock (but maybe prefers to flower elsewhere).

"His last novel brims with unusual optimism as well as his customary wit. For an author of 72 to have invented such a credible teenage girl is remarkable...; What Hetty Did *is like the first breath of spring."*

Amanda Craig, *Sunday Express*

"This book, generally so witty, so vivacious and so original, is a gem."

Francis King, *The Spectator*

ISBN 0-900847-91-3